Forbidden Fruit

A Novel

PAMELA PUJO

PENDULUM
PUBLISHING

Originally published by Svelte Books in 2008. The original edition is no longer available.

Published in the United States by Pendulum Publishing, McKinney, Texas.
Email: pen_publishing@sbcglobal.net

Forbidden Fruit: A Novel / by Pamela Pujo. – 2nd ed.

ISBN: 0-9789826-1-4
ISBN-13: 978-0-9789826-1-4

Cover art by Kingsley Onyeiwu

DEDICATION

To my family and friends who are near and far, who have guided,
supported and uplifted me through the years.

"…to bestow on them a crown of beauty instead of ashes, the oil of gladness instead of mourning, and a garment of praise instead of a spirit of despair." Isaiah 61:3

CHAPTER 1 - COOL BEGINNINGS

Surrounded by a sea of white and enveloped in the ambience of the glow of clear lights, Jackie sashayed into the grand ballroom of the posh Hotel Piedmont. It was early December, cool and crisp outside, but warm and festive inside, as the Dallas socialites mixed and mingled at the social event of the year. Light laughter filled the air as partygoers schmoozed, laughed, and chatted at the annual Black and White Charity Ball which kicked off the festive holiday season.

The foyer glistened with twinkling white lights, elegantly draped around rows of freshly cut pine trees and snow-like cotton blanketed the base of the cone-shaped foliage creating the allusion of a winter wonderland. Christmas classics, reformatted to a jazz melody, floated throughout the ballroom. Servers graciously moved about carrying trays of sparkling champagne and dainty hors d'oeuvres.

For the festive occasion, Jackie spared no expense on her shopping excursion at The Galleria. She purchased the perfect black floor-length gown which was sprinkled with slivers of metallic silver thread. The gown's silk flowed effortlessly around her petite frame and the thin rhinestone straps caressed her shoulders. The low scooped back exposed her smooth pecan-colored skin. She adorned her earlobes with princess cut diamond stud earrings and draped her neck with a matching diamond pendant necklace. Her hairstylist had curled and combed Jackie's long black hair into a flowing masterpiece. Her trip to the Elegant Nail Salon added the finishing touches of Blossom Cherry nail polish; adding the final perfect touch for the elegant evening.

Jackie Weston, an advertising executive with the top-rated firm of Wellington and Wellington, had always dreamed of attending a fancy function since childhood. Her dream came true when her director, Herbert Bell, surprised her with a ticket to the charity fundraiser.

Jackie sipped on a glass of champagne and nibbled on a wheat cracker topped with a miniature piece of smoked salmon, a pinch of cream cheese, and sprinkled with chives. The winter wonderland provided an escape from Jackie's past frustrations, present imperfections, and future worries. Lost in thought, she did not notice Mr. Bell dressed in his tuxedo waddling towards her with his overexcited wife in tow. He was always poised with an air of importance.

"Jackie, how are you enjoying the evening so far?" Mr. Bell asked. His voice boomed with a distinctive bass tone like a famed television show host. He respected Jackie for her hard work, dedication, and creativity.

"It's fabulous. Thanks for the invite." Jackie admired the distinctive look that Mr. Bell possessed, his salt and pepper hair, mustache trimmed to perfection, and creased forehead implanted with years of wisdom. "Hello, Mrs. Bell. How are you this evening?" Jackie stated flashing her perfectly-lined pearly white teeth.

"Wonderful, Jackie. It's nice to see you this evening," Mrs. Bell politely responded with her light voice. The contrast between her and Mr. Bell was so evident. He was enormously masculine and she extremely feminine. He hovered over everyone at six feet tall and she barely measured up to five feet.

Herbert chimed in with an ego-boosting comment, "Not a

problem for one of my best workers. Keep up the good work and some big accounts will come sailing your way."

Jackie's face glowed with delight. Lately, her guardian angel was guiding her down destiny's path at an unbelievable speed. She felt like a speeding ticket would be issued at this fast pace; however, she was not complaining. She had come a long way from the small, rural town of Creekwater, Florida. She was not about to make a U-turn.

The socialites dressed in their flowing ball gowns and tuxedoes flowed into the grand ballroom for the four-course dinner. The round tables resembled stars sparkling in an indigo night sky, dotted across the dark blue carpet. Jackie's table was positioned off center from the dais allowing her a bird's-eye view of the entire room. Her director and his wife took their seats at the same table.

"The sad thing about these events is that the food is usually less than par," Mr. Bell remarked as he laid his dinner napkin in his lap. "Always make sure you eat something early or you'll starve by night's end."

"Oh, Herbert stop complaining," Mrs. Bell chided her husband. She was just thankful for a night out and away from the usual routine of home alone, even though Herbert was usually hibernating in his study. Twenty-eight years of marriage and there was only a faint flicker of romance glowing. She could count the days on one hand when their evenings were infused with excitement – birthdays, anniversary, Christmas – the big three.

Waiting to be served, Jackie unconsciously shifted the silverware of her place setting so that the edges of the forks and knife perfectly aligned themselves like tin soldiers in battle formation. Annoying perfection was her trademark. Finally, the servers brought the first course of the evening meal, a field green salad with raspberry vinaigrette.

The empty seat to her right puzzled Jackie. She thought *why would anyone pay a hundred dollars for a plate and then do a disappearing act.* She hoped someone appear sooner or later, rather sooner, to close the hole in the loop of diners around the table. Her curiosity sat on edge all night wandering who is the mystery person. And besides, she did not know how much longer she could bear to hear Mrs. Bell chat about the past twenty-eight years she has dealt with Herbert's annoying habits; socks sprawled on the floor, a dirty glass in the sink, shaving cream splattered on the mirror, the Sunday newspaper spread across the family room floor as Herbert shouted at the football players on the big screen TV like he was the NFL head coach. *Twenty-eight years.*

Herbert nudged his wife and whispered through tight lips, "Do you have to tell all of my personal business? After all, she is my employee, not my soon to be next wife." He thought, *and she wonders why I don't take her anywhere. I'm sorry I forgot the muzzle.*

Jackie was barely out of earshot from hearing Mr. Bell chide his wife for her tournament of tongue wagging and jaw flapping. She definitely would have been a first place winner in the tournament of pets. The main course, classic grilled chicken garnished with a cream Dijon sauce along with steamed vegetables, was being served when the last of Jackie's tablemates arrived. *How rude* she thought as the smooth maple-colored skin, dark-haired gentleman eased into the chair next to her. His muted arrogance was a well-worn resemblance of the way he wore his black tuxedo – easy. Kevin Carlisle's reputation, for tardiness, was knowledgably absent from the circle of diners. In Kevin's mind, the world revolved around his time; he controlled the hour, the minute, and the second hand. Kevin was the moneyman with all the answers to any financial dilemma. He worked his way up to Senior Investment Banker, at Infinity Financial Solutions, by mastering deal after deal generating millions for the startup company.

"Hello. Excuse me for my tardiness," Kevin stated only as a courtesy, not really concerned if he offended anyone.

"Hello, how are you this evening?" Jackie replied while looking at Kevin from out of the corner of her eye.

"Wonderful. I just finished a huge investment deal," he stated with modest pride. "My name is Kevin Carlisle. What is your name young lady?"

"Jackie Weston. That's interesting about your business deal," Jackie replied with a cool casualness, thinking *how arrogant. Who goes around boasting about their business dealings to a complete stranger?*

Kevin admired the beauty and grace of his lovely tablemate. He sensed that she was either introverted or imperceptive by her short and to the point responses.

He tried to make light of the evening by passing time with some stale jokes. "What does the dinner rolls remind you of?" Kevin asked Jackie jokingly.

"Bread," Jackie said matter-of-factly while holding her hands slightly in the air.

"Bread! You're so right." *Will she ever respond with a complete sentence or even add some excitement to her tone. Please don't tell me all beauty and no brains*, Kevin thought.

"They look like baseballs to me; even feels hard like one!"

Jackie smiled a polite smile, and thought *a man's mind is either thinking about sports or sex. I wonder if they can ever stretch their imagination.* She then laughed at his corny, but cute joke anyway.

The servers cleared the tables of the plates even though the majority of them still possessed large portions of the expensive cuisine. As dessert and coffee were served, the keynote speaker, Representative Clarice Wharton, moved to the podium to deliver her speech to instill encouragement and to offer enlightenment. The partygoers were moved to an awaken consciousness as well as entertained by Representative Wharton's speech.

"I urge everyone to focus their energies to uplift and reach back into the community. Reach back and pull someone up along with you. I encourage you to focus on your goals and to embrace each day."

The audience applauded at those key moments as Representative Wharton continued with her motivating words of wisdom. Jackie's attention faded in and out while she attempted to look interested. She wanted to tally up as many browning points as the evening allowed.

After all, extra points with the boss never hurt. She always went for the extra point, starting in grade school as the teacher's pet.

"I cannot stress enough that education is the foundation upon which greatness is built. I cannot stress enough how knowledge equals power beyond measure. My friends remember success is not an individual journey, but a collective one. Success is the pinnacle point in a step-by-step process of reaching one's goals. Success is learning from your failures and pressing on toward fulfillment of your goals." Jackie zoned in on the words "success is learning from your failures." The words resonated through her mind. They played over and over like a scratched album. She did not like to fail; only perfection sufficed.

Jackie was jolted from her wide-eyed daydream when a feather-like touch moved along her hand. Kevin's subtle movements created a chill which was mixed with a pleasantly warm tingly sensation that traveled down her spine.

"What wonderland were you living in?" Kevin asked with a wide smile flashing his perfect row of pearly whites.

"Oh, just thinking about the speaker's comment on success and failure," Jackie commented nonchalantly.

"Well, I know a thing or two about success," Kevin remarked with puffed up pride. "I'm ranked as the number one broker in my territory." He pointed at his chest to add emphasis to his revered ranking.

"What type of broker are you?"

"An investment banker," Kevin replied with a polished smile.

"Interesting. That's right you did mention something about an investment deal earlier this evening."

Jackie did not want to give the impression that she was too interested. But her almond-shaped eyes had already zoned in on the latecomer's ring finger, out of habit. When fate places an attractive man in your path, might as well take advantage of the opportunity. No shining gold or silvery platinum; no tan line marked the spot. A cautious smile curled upon her lips as she questionably thought, *is*

God smiling on me, or what?

"Hey, enough talk about business. The band has set up and is kicking off some funky jazz tunes. How about a dance with a brother?"

Jackie hoped fate would not be that cruel to steer a smart, sexy, and single man in her direction, only to have him change into a frog at the stroke of midnight. Her heart danced a step of its own as Kevin's warm hand pressed on her exposed back, and sent a surge of energy to her heart. Jackie thought *why did he have to touch me with those soft, warm hands; hands that possessed heat that penetrated to the bone?*

Jackie and Kevin zigzagged their way to the makeshift, brown square which was set up to pose as a dance floor. They joined the other couples, who were lit up with champagne, to twirl and swing on the tiny square. The band switched to a slow melody with a soft beat as the pair approached the dance floor. Kevin smiled and hunched his shoulders at Jackie as to say *Oh well, we're here now. Might as well make the most of it.* She did not mind a slow dance that provided her the opportunity to gaze into his blazing brown eyes. She noticed how his eyes seemed to twinkle at the right time when he looked at her.

The night progressed as the two laughed and danced. Jackie had not noticed how the time had slipped away, and she had church services to attend tomorrow morning.

"It's getting late and I have to wake up early for church. It was nice meeting you."

Kevin's mind shifted into play mode, *get the number.* "Hey do you mind if I call you?"

"Of course not," Jackie stated while her heart danced some more and a quiet *Thank you God* filled her mind. "Here is my business card."

"Great, I'll call you."

CHAPTER 2 – CAFÉ RENDEZVOUS

Tiffany Guillory gazed across the crowded café. She was not really focused on anything or anyone in particular; just caught up in a daydream. Thoughts circulated throughout her mind of the upcoming holidays. She was oblivious to the light-skinned gentleman, with the piercing deep brown eyes who watched her from across the crowded café. The only thought that crossed Tiffany's mind was the yummy pasta salad she wanted to savor. She inched closer to the register as the line progressed like a snail crawling across a busy highway. Café Swirl, the trendy restaurant with its cosmopolitan flare, was the hot spot for the downtown lunch crew. They offered a menu to satisfy the hearty meat-lover or the finicky vegetarian. The restaurant's décor was blasted with a chic palette of bold colors splashed throughout the restaurant.

"How may I help you?" the guy with gel-spiked hair said, nonchalantly from behind the steel counter. His black uniform-like attire enhanced his somber attitude. Tiffany snapped out of her trance and recited her order like she was reciting her lines in a movie. "I'll have the pasta chicken salad and an ice tea."

"Ok. Your total is $12.58. The red lights on the gizmo will flash when your order is ready. Thank you. Next," he mouthed with hollow enthusiasm. *Amazing how robotic our society sounds and moves*, Tiffany thought, *but how much can a person enjoy repeating the same words day after day.*

Tiffany dropped the change in her wallet, picked up the gizmo, and moved to a table near the picture window so she could gaze out at the waterfall and spiky green palm trees. A calming oasis nestled in the heart of the inner city that blocked out the jumbled noise of honking horns and loud-talking pedestrians. She jotted down gifts to her growing Christmas list; diamond earrings for Mom, perfume for Aunt Diane, pajamas for cousin Shauntay, and a sweater for Jackie. The mystery eyes continued to observe her and mentally soak in her beauty. He admired her pale blond hair falling past her shoulders, her thin waistline leading to her full hips, her vanilla-colored skin with a scoop of chocolate, and the tantalizing features of her face. Her beauty turned many heads as well as occasionally causing intrigue about her nationality.

Her mother was Creole and her absent father lived on the side of the tracks where the light-skinned folks resided. Tiffany never met her father, only heard about him. He was a young lawyer who worked in the District Attorney's office in the city of Lafayette.

Tiffany was as fair-skinned as any Caucasian woman. A few freckles splashed across the tips of her nose that laid a path to each rosy cheek. Her hair was long and a dusty pale blonde. Her eyes were hazel and sparkled in the reflection of the light. Her beauty caused her blessings and curses. As a little girl growing up in the rural South, her fair-skinned complexion afforded her many advantages that her darker-skinned friends were not privileged to experience.

Tiffany's mother, Luella, worked many years at Petre's Cajun Café in Lafayette. The café occupied a corner in the heart of the small downtown square which was a couple of blocks from the old courthouse. Tiffany's father made it a mission to visit Petre's every time he had a hearing at the historic courthouse. He was ambitious, ready to take on the world, but not ready to take on a family.

However, he could not fight the instant infatuation with Luella. Tiffany inherited her mother's glowing beauty. Every time Tiffany's father made a trip to the café, he sat at the same table in the corner where he knew Luella was the waitress du jour. He ordered the same meal each time; blackened catfish, Cole slaw, hushpuppies, and a side of Petre's famous dirty rice. For dessert, he requested black coffee and peach cobbler; even though, swirling around in his mind was always the thought of having Luella for dessert. Her pale blue uniform, with her freshly starched apron, clung to her petite body which was shaped like a bowling pin. He was spontaneously infatuated with Luella. The twinkle in his eyes and the easy curve of his lips into a smile, at each sighting of her, would have proved him a liar, if he said otherwise.

The lights flashed, like a flying saucer on the square gadget, and danced with a buzzing sound on the slate tabletop. Tiffany picked up the gadget and walked to the steel counter to finally pick up her pasta salad. She moved graciously through the maze of tables mapping out the shortest route possible. Along that route, the deep brown-eyed gentleman pushed his chair out to stand up and conveniently block her path.

"Excuse me. I'm sorry. I didn't see you walking by," Robert apologized with a warm smile plastered across his chiseled face. His dark chocolate eyes warmed with a twinkle as he gazed into Tiffany's hazel eyes.

"Oh, excuse me. I didn't see you."

"I hope I didn't spill anything on your lovely pink sweater." His expression was filled with empathy and apologies, while knowingly admiring her beauty from head to toe.

"No, I'm fine, really. This little stain will come out easy." Tiffany wanted to move on, but he blocked her path like a defensive end positioned in front of a running back, steady and unyielding.

"My name is Robert. Please take my business card and let me pay for the dry cleaning charges. It is the least I can do." He looked like a sorrowful puppy whose owner had just scolded him for wetting on the newly laid carpet. She accepted the card graciously, smiled and tried to move on.

Tiffany smiled a warm smile, not wanting to be forceful; but her food was slowly turning into a cold pasta salad and not the hot chicken and pasta that she had been dreaming about.

"If the bill costs a lot, I'll call you. Thank you, but I only have an hour for lunch, so if you'll excuse me." She nudged forward and he unwillingly moved to the side allowing her to make a move. She finally reached her table, ate her lunch, and completed her Christmas list. The hour was almost up and she did not want to have to give an explanation to her supervisor about a longer than usual lunch.

The unrelenting businessman that Robert was, he could not leave the café without closing the deal and securing the phone number of the lady in pink. He watched Tiffany like he was a birdwatcher eyeing a prized peacock. Her every move was in plain view of his imaginary binoculars. As she finished her meal, he timed his last play down to the last second. He had no more timeouts remaining. She headed for the door and Robert made his move.

"Looks like we're meant to keep bumping into each other," he stated casually as he reached the door at the same time as Tiffany.

"It looks that way," Tiffany said trying to make her move in a different direction. *I know he is going to ask me for my phone number,* Tiffany thought while her lips remained pursed together and her shoulders hunched up with tension.

"Do you mind if I have your phone number? You are a very pretty lady. Maybe we can have lunch together sometime."

"Maybe. I don't eat out for lunch that often. My work schedule is very busy." *Hopefully, he will get the hint,* Tiffany thought with an ounce of hope.

"Come on. All work makes for a dull Jane."

"My name is Tiffany, not Jane." *Darn. I gave him my real name. I broke rule number one, no real names.*

"Do you have a business card?" He persistently pressed. After all, he was not known as the deal-closer for nothing. She reached into her purse and found a business card bearing her company's logo, McDougal Sterling, her name, her work number, and her email address; everything he needed to contact her at any given moment. She reluctantly passed him the card. His stocky fingers lightly grazed her long, skinny manicured hand as she passed her card to him. In his mind, he had scored a touchdown. In her mind, he was running towards the wrong goal line.

CHAPTER 3 - DEEP WOUNDS

The Sunday morning hallelujah aerobic workout church services worked up an appetite in the longtime friends, Jackie and Tiffany. New Tabernacle Missionary Baptist church was well known for its spirited jumps and shouts, clap your hands and stomp your feet, body jerking and head bouncing worship services. Anyone perched on the pew, and did not even as much fly a feather, had to be deaf, dumb, or just plain dead in the spirit. Pastor Ray Dalton, with his famous swing high, swing low rhythm-like preaching, moved even the chief of sinners toward salvation. And with his backup doo-wop choir – tears, jerks, and unexplainable sporadic body movements were sure to abound. New Tabernacle also resonated with history.

The edifice was constructed in 1896 by a small group of humble servants wanting to worship the Lord in the way the Spirit moved them. The church still maintained its original body structure with a few minor repairs and upgrades. The stained-glass windows were etched with images of Christ, standing glorified in the Jordan River, with three crosses stretched wide on Calvary's hill which overlooked the worshippers each Sunday morning. The weathered bell hung in the steeple ringing loud and clear, calling the gathering of the great cloud of witnesses to testify to the strength of their faith.

Jackie and Tiffany decided, after their first meeting, that their friendship was destined to always ring true. The duo had been inseparable since their sophomore year when they were college roommates at East Louisiana Tech University. They shared secrets, hopes, and dreams like they were sisters from birth. They shared heartaches, breakups, and setbacks. Both were only children; not knowing the complexities of sibling rivalry or the joys of sisterly love.

After the religious revelry stopped, the benediction was spoken and the usual hellos of fellowship were exchanged, they drove to their usual after Sunday services brunch spot, Sister Soul's. The soul food, honey glazed ham, macaroni and cheese, sweet potatoes, collard greens, cornbread, and a tall glass of sweet ice tea, were just like mama's home cooked meals. Both girls had roots from the sunny South. Jackie was raised and reared in Creekwater, Florida and Tiffany blossomed in Sunset Bayou, Louisiana.

The wait at Sister Soul's, an upscale locale with a down home flavor, was always at least thirty minutes allowing the twosome time to recap and reenact the morning's worship service.

"Girl, Pastor Dalton preached this morning," Tiffany remarked.

"You know he did. When doesn't he? Sometimes I don't understand the message, but he sounds good," Jackie said with the innocence of a baby born-again Christian. Only twenty-six years old, she worked on growing spiritually and increasing her walk of faith. She attempted to build upon the Christian foundation that her grandmother instilled in her many years ago.

"And he looks too good. You have to give it to him and Sister Dalton. She is one lucky lady." Tiffany and Jackie sighed in unison like a choir meditating on the handsome masculinity of their middle-aged pastor.

"Well, I met someone who maybe *my* Pastor Dalton, even though I didn't sense anything religious about him; but he looks good," Jackie bragged.

"Oh, are you holding out on a sistah?" Tiffany gave her a side look. "What's the low down on Mr. Look-So-Good?"

The hostess, with a quick interruption of their conversation, showed the ladies to their table. The table was angled to form a diamond shape, layered with a starched white tablecloth surrounded by black lacquered chairs, near the front of the restaurant. The fuchsia Gerber Daisy stood proudly in the miniature vase and reflected a splash of color like a prism that glowed in the sunlight. Their table was in a prime location for a Sunday, since Sister's was the after church gathering spot to be seen. The Sunday gospel brunch presented the grand finale of amen's and hallelujah's from the morning's Holy Ghost showcase of puppet parishioners. The pianist played the shiny black piano with fluid fingers. The soloist sang sweet, heavenly melodies as the diners cherished each delicious morsel.

Jackie replayed a meticulous account of last week's meeting for Tiffany like an instant replay for a professional football game; play-by-play, with embellished commentary. Of course, Jackie's details were precise – smooth caramel skin, coal black eyes, soft lips, firm but soft hands, and a body that connected with hers in all the right places. Jackie had the bait to catch this fish, but somehow the big ones always slipped away. She was determined to not only bait the big fish, but to reel him in for the long haul. She knew, in her heart and soul, that Kevin was the one to walk down that aisle leading to marital bliss. Prayers had poured out with tears streaming down her face only a few nights earlier. God answered this prayer quickly. She was not going to let Him down – again.

"At least you met somebody decent," Tiffany chimed in after hearing enough about Mr. Fabulous. "You know my luck with men – nonexistent."

"Come on, Tiff. You've met some good guys, at least one," Jackie tried to sound encouraging. Older men were Tiffany's main attraction. She was always searching for the proverbial father figure. The man who would turn off the flashing neon vacant sign that hung over her heart; a brightly colored neon sign that spelled out *Lonely and*

Rejected.

"Whatever, girl. Which one are you thinking about?" Tiffany eyed her best friend with a look of skepticism. "Anyway, this man was intent on making the play to run a numbers game," Tiffany commented.

"Did you give up the digits?" Jackie asked curiously as she sat straight up in the black lacquered chair.

"Reluctantly, I gave him my business card." Tiffany still felt indifferent toward the encounter. There was warmth in the chocolate eyes that somehow connected with her, but still an uneasy feeling loomed in the pit of her stomach. The uneasy feeling that is felt when a storm is on the way.

"What's wrong with him?" Jackie had a puzzled look across her face.

"He's too stubby, too old, and the list goes on," Tiffany stated disappointedly.

Jackie was thankful when the waitress walked up and interrupted their conversation which was turning into a mudslide; all downhill. She placed two ice waters, with lemon, on the table and a basket of hot bread, with soft butter in a small dish, to appease the hungry diners. The soul food pacified not only the hunger pains, but the pains of loneliness, the pains of rejection, and the pains of missing the comfort of home. The waitress, proudly sporting her micro-braided locks with kente-cloth twisted into a makeshift headband, jotted down their orders and then strode off to the kitchen.

Jackie had no response to Tiffany's headline news, only a nod of the head as she quickly sipped her water to disguise her uneasiness. She hoped that one day Tiffany moved past the distress and rejection of not knowing her father. She understood the depth of Tiffany's loneliness and dejection. After all, she had only known her parents for twelve short years. Her parents were killed in a car crash when Jackie was on a summer visit at Grandma Meme's in Creekwater. Jackie's visits to Grandma Meme for the summer months started when she was eight years old, just after Grandpa Felix had suffered a fatal heart attack and went home to Heaven. Her parents were traveling a two lane East Texas highway, in the early morning hours, on their way to Creekwater to collect their only baby girl, since summer vacation had come to a close, when a sleepy driver swerved into their lane hitting them head on. The crash was quick and fatal. Jackie became a permanent resident of Creekwater, staying more than just summers with Grandma Meme from that tragic moment forward.

Jackie shifted gears, in the now cheerless conversation, to a gear that was even gloomier. Her nights were restless with perplexing dreams: dreams that caused tears to form in the corners of her eyes, dreams that brought a quickened pulse and a rapid heartbeat, dreams that brought a cold sweat in the dead of night. She recounted the vivid details of the annoying dreams etched in her mind. The odious dreams were of a miserly midget man with wild, wooly hair, jagged teeth, flaky skin, tattered clothes, and a heinous laugh. Jackie's brain could not purge the poisonous words that spewed from his foul mouth. He laughed and pointed at Jackie shouting, '*I got you now, I got you now*' as she stood frozen like a chiseled ice sculpture. Retelling the dream sent a shiver of coldness through her soul as if she had crossed the grave of an angry spirit.

"What do you think it means?" Jackie asked with desperate curiosity.

"It either foretells of the future or dirt from the grave has been disturbed," Tiffany spoke the words as if they were not her own words, but words of an ancient soul. She always thought of herself as someone with an old soul and a young heart. Tiffany would sit perched on the weathered wooden stool in the corner of the small pea-green kitchen - listening and watching Grandma Tizzy work her magic to interpret the dreams of the townspeople. Grandma Tizzy poised with a mysterious demeanor would stretch out her pale pink hands with her palms face up across the table. She would close her eyes as she listened to the dream retold by the curious parishioner. After a moment of silence, she would suddenly open her hazy gray eyes and gaze at the individual seated across from her would speak the words of the future.

Folks from all over Arcadia Parish flocked to have Ms. Tizzy predict the meaning of their dreams for only five dollars. Grandma Tizzy collected her hard-earned money and kept it secure in a glass mason jar hidden in the pantry. The waitress skillfully balanced the heavy tray carrying the mouth-watering entrees. The delicious aroma of the home cooking piled on the platter-sized plates aroused Tiffany from her altered state of mind.

"Ok girl. Enough with the doom and gloom," Tiffany sighed.

"You're right. Besides this food looks like the bomb," Jackie remarked before bowing her head to say grace.

"On a much lighter note, did you see Sister Armstrong break down?" Tiffany exclaimed.

"Girl, Sister Armstrong knows she is wrong," Jackie stated while performing a watered down version of the church lady. "Jumping and shouting every Sunday; it's the same thing."

"Her breakthrough can't get through to find her," Tiffany laughed. "The noise from either her shouts or the bells on the one arm bandits is too noisy. You know she has a gambling problem?"

"How did you find that out?" Jackie asked.

"Girl, one Sunday, while in the lady's room, I was freshening up my makeup and Sister Armstrong walks in, sporting her usual holy-thou-art attitude, and offers a good morning smirk. Well she accidentally dropped her purse and the contents spilled out all over the floor. Her Chantilly perfume bottle, outdated pressed powder, and what you do know...tokens from the casino!"

"Shut up!" Jackie exclaimed.

"She was rushing and scurrying around, trying to collect her belongings, especially those prized tokens. I handed her the ten dollar token that rolled across the floor while I tried to keep a straight face. She said, 'Baby, now this isn't for me. It belongs to my son. He likes to drive over to Shreveport from time to time, and well, he dropped it on the sofa while visiting one day.'"

"She was lying in church," Jackie stated. Her eyes were opened wide with disbelief.

"The holy-roller was lying and flying out of the restroom quicker than the cherry's spin on the slot machine."

"Girl, I'm sorry, but I would not have been able to look at her with a straight face."

"Trust me, every time I see her, it takes the strength of Jesus for me not to laugh," Tiffany said with a wide smile.

"Now, young lady you'd better quit talkin 'bout folks," Jackie said with an imitation of her grandmother's scolding.

CHAPTER 4 – LITTLE THINGS

The pink roses sat elegantly on Tiffany's desk. The note scribbled on the card said *Thinking of you.* Her mind raced back and forth, *who could have sent her the flowers, so simple yet graceful.* Not once had she even considered the gentleman from the café; maybe someone from church or in the office. The businessman was a distant memory, and his card was thrown in the trash. Memories of the past flooded Tiffany's mind. The pink flowers reminded her of the dainty pink handkerchief that Mama stored away in her Sunday purse.

Tiffany had come a long way from her hometown of Sunset Bayou. A town with only a four-way stop sign to serve as the major intersection and only one of everything that served as a necessity – a gas station, a corner market, a beauty parlor, a barber shop, and a police station which had as much action as the jail in the town of Mayberry. For some other things, Sunset had nothing to offer. Tiffany and her schoolmates were bused to the nearby city of Lafayette to receive their first-rate education. And there were some other things Sunset possessed too much of. Any religious denomination could pick a spot and setup shop. The Baptist had Sunset Baptist church, which was not named after the town. It was named after the fact that church services did not end until the sunset. The Methodist had New Zion A.M.E. church and the Catholics had Holy Cross Catholic church.

Monday morning dragged and stalled. The accounts that she received were mediocre, routine and mundane. Tiffany sat at the slate gray desk tapping her pen mindlessly as she stared, with a blank expression, at the computer monitor reflecting on the past years. Tiffany mentally observed the miles she had traveled to arrive at her current destination. Many small steps lined the path with a pattern of two steps forward and one step backward.

Tiffany had finally landed her dream event planning job after several short-term gigs. McDougal Sterling provided a long-term feel, which was full of perks and fun extras. It was, hopefully, a clear shot to the top. This was Tiffany's golden opportunity to finally show off her hot creative skills. She seized the opportunity to spread her wings and let the pains and disappointments of the past fly away into the blue sky. She mustered the determination to step outside of the confinements of the four-sided personal prison comprised of inhibitions, shyness, bashfulness, and fearfulness. She only had to work her way up the slippery slopes of corporate America's ladder. The company, large and running in the race with top firms across the country, was a breeding ground for vulture's vying their way to the top spot and picking away at their counterparts like a carcass in the dessert.

Tiffany's supervisor, Mary Beth Daigle decked out in her navy blue pinstripe pantsuit, walked into her miniature makeshift office and handed her another account, jolting her out of the hazy daydream of childhood memories.

"Tiffany, I'm assigning you the account for the Promise Keepers charity luncheon," Mary Beth announced.

"Great. I've always admired the organization. They do such great work in the community," Tiffany commented.

"True and this luncheon is a major fundraising event for them. They usually bring in around $500,000 in donations," Mary Beth stated matter-of-factly. At the same time, Tiffany could not help but wonder what she did to have favor fall upon her; as if Mary Beth was reading her mind.

"I like the job you did on the Eastland Prep account. I want to stretch your talent. I see potential in your work. Keep up the good work," Mary Beth remarked.

"Thank you for the complement. I'll get started right away," Tiffany mouthed with a plastered professional smile.

"Oh, by the way, I'm a board member for Promise Keepers, so don't make me look bad," Mary Beth said with a raised eyebrow just before leaving Tiffany's office.

After Mary Beth left, Tiffany said a quick, *thank you and help me, God.* She knew this account was a 'make me or break me' once-in-a-lifetime chance, especially since her supervisor was closely affiliated with the organization. Tiffany knew, from hearing several sermons, God knows the desires of our hearts, and since she had not had a chance to officially pray for her desires, receiving this account proved that God was listening to her heart.

Tiffany flipped through the folder of information to familiarize herself with the contents, while still joyfully reflecting on God's perfect timing. As a young Christian, she was still working on trust and believing God's promises in His Word. Mama always told her to trust God with all her heart. Trusting people eluded Tiffany and trusting God was on a different playing field. How could she trust and believe, let alone hope that something, anything good would come her way? The rejection by her father ruled out trust. The fear of rejection radiated constantly through her thoughts. The very thing she constantly feared showed up in her life. Rejection had taken root and the only way to weed it out was to plant new seed. The season was ripe for harvesting abundance, love, and joy -- just the way Pastor Dalton had preached during yesterday's sermon.

Back home, Tiffany was a member of Holy Cross Catholic Church. The one-hour long Mass never captured her attention. Without the standing, sitting, and kneeling workout, she definitely would have slept her way to Heaven. Tiffany remembered making her first communion, at the tender age of eight years old, dressed in her pristine white cotton dress with a dainty lace overlay. Her white bobby socks were trimmed with scalloped lace edges and tucked into her white patent-leather Mary Jane shoes. She remembered how Mama smiled a huge grin, as she dabbed away the tears with her pink handkerchief, while Tiffany marched into the church laden with statutes of the Virgin Mary and the Saints. Tiffany smiled at Mama with a quick grin keeping her hands in the prayer position as instructed by Sister Catherine.

Tiffany wore the prettiest clothes as a little girl. Mama always made certain that her little girl had the finest of everything. Tiffany remembered the soothing, loving words that Mama shared with her that first communion morning as she brushed and curled her long locks.

"Mama, this is a pretty dress," Tiffany commented in her soft child's voice.

"It is a pretty dress for a very pretty and special little girl," Luella said as she placed a hand on each of Tiffany's cheeks. "Remember baby, you are always special and you are loved."

"Yes, Mama. I'll remember." Tiffany never gave a thought how Mama could afford to pay for all the pretty clothes.

The receptionist buzzed Tiffany's line. She answered placing the coveted folder with her new assignment on her desk and putting her thoughts of yesteryear behind her.

Tiffany picked the telephone receiver. "This is Tiffany Guillory. How may I help you?"

"Hello. This is Robert Carrington from the café last week." The smile on his face was as wide the Mississippi River.

"Oh yes, hello. How are you?" Tiffany stated with a hint of annoyance in her voice.

"Great. I waited for you to call me about the dry cleaning bill."

"You didn't have to worry about the bill. The amount was minimal. I paid for it." She tapped her pen annoyingly on her desk.

"Allow me to take you to lunch to make up for it." Robert leaned back in his black leather executive chair.

"Really, you don't have to. It wasn't a problem." Tiffany was desperately thinking of something to say to quickly end the phone call.

"Did you receive the flowers this morning?" He swiveled his chair around to gaze out the glass window overlooking the downtown skyline. The mid-morning sun gleamed and reflected off the steel office towers.

"Yes, the pink roses. They are beautiful." A smile crept across Tiffany's face. She quickly tried to dismiss it.

"For a beautiful lady," Robert commented with his lips curled with a sly grin. "How can you say no, especially after the smile I've put on your face."

"Well for your information, I'm not smiling. And I can still say no to lunch. But I'll say thank you for the lovely flowers."

Tiffany wished he would just disappear, but then he mentioned the restaurant Chez Gumbeaux, she put her hesitations aside and accepted the invitation. She heard the food was delicious enough to taste like the authentic Creole cooking like her mama's. After all, a few weeks would pass before she drove the many hours to her hometown to feast on Mama's delicious cooking and all the fixings for the Christmas holidays. And besides, it was only lunch, one time. She hoped the lunch date appeased him and her wish of him disappearing would be granted.

The morning of their lunch date, Tiffany agonized over what to wear. She debated back and forth over something ultra conservative or something casual. After all, she did not want to give him the impression that she was the least bit interested and no ammunition to entice him to continue pursuing her. She opted for her interview attire, her black business suit and crisp white blouse. If this outfit, did say business only, then she did not know else would do the trick. She combed her hair into a tight bun like her fifth-grade teacher wore.

However, she noticed that there was a small part of her that was nervous and excited about meeting Robert again. She always held onto that ounce of hope that something good would happen sooner or later. She realized that oftentimes, God would put a person or situation in someone's life that eventually would lead to destiny. She held onto to the possibility that their chance meeting was the start of the path towards something greater.

She arrived at her office earlier than usual. Without the buzz of office machinery and coworker chatter, the morning silence proved to be lonely. Tiffany walked to the coffee machine in the break room and selected a large café mocha. She hoped the java would help soothe her nervousness. She and mama would enjoy coffee on Saturday mornings with large breakfast of scrambled eggs, bacon, and grits. But this morning, there was no luck in calming her nerves.

She seemed to become even more fidgety as the morning progressed. She flipped aimlessly through files, tapped the keys on her computer, played with the computer mouse, and for the most part, stared at the monitor. She opened the file for the Promise Keepers account and reviewed her to do list, nothing had been checked off. Usually, she was ahead of the game, but with the holidays coming up and the Robert lunch date, her mind was miles away from work. She promised her self at the beginning of the year, she would focus and put her self back on track.

The lunch hour had arrived. She gathered her purse and walked to the garage. She hopped into her black Mazda and zigzagged her way out of the garage. She drove up to the valet parking station at Chez Gumbeaux, and then walked into the lobby area. She walked up to the maître d' and informed her that she meeting a gentleman, Robert Carrington, for lunch. The maître d' scrolled through her reservation list and then guided Tiffany to the round corner booth where Robert sat waiting. He donned an Armani dark chocolate suit with a gold-speckled tie. His wiry black hair was cropped close, his mustache was neatly trimmed, and his fingernails were perfectly manicured.

Robert stood up and extended his hand to guide Tiffany where to sit, "Hello young lady, it's very nice to see you again."

"Hello, Mr. Carrington. Thank you again for the invitation," Tiffany mouthed as she nervously scooted into the burgundy leather booth.

"Please call me Robert. There is no need formality. After all this is a friendly lunch date," Robert smiled at Tiffany with a twinkle in his eye.

"A lunch meeting as a piece offering for the dry cleaning issue, nothing more," Tiffany remarked sternly. She moved to a location in the booth to ensure ample space was between them.

"You're too pretty of a young lady to be so rigid. It appears that you're not interested in getting to know each other. Maybe by the end of this lunch, I'll have changed your mind." He sat cool and confident like a lion ruling his jungle.

Tiffany laid the white cotton napkin in her lap and wiped her sweaty palms. She opened her menu. "What do you suggest is a good dish?" She asked to change the subject. She wanted to order, eat, and leave.

"I like the spicy crawfish etouffeé." Robert replied hoping to warm things up. He noticed that she was nervous.

"I love etouffeé. I'm from Louisiana, so I'll see if their version measures up." Tiffany commented. She started to relax. It seems like they may have something in common, food at the most part. She had noticed he was a bit on the chunky side, which gave a clear indication that he was a lover of food.

The pair nibbled on their entrees and playfully chatted throughout the lunch hour. By the end of the meal, Tiffany had warmed up to Robert. His funny sense of humor helped her to relax and enjoy his company. She was still somewhat apprehensive, but only because of his age. The signs of aging creased across his forehead and drew tiny lines at the corners of his eyes.

"Tiffany may I see you again? Maybe we can have a standing

lunch date, or do you still prefer to call it a meeting? I enjoyed your company. And like me, you seem to enjoy good food and good company," Robert flashed his dazzling white smile and rubbed his necktie. His charming personality proved to be irresistible for Tiffany. She admired the dimples that formed in his checks each time he smiled.

"Lunch date sounds just fine. And yes, I would like that very much," She responded smiling from ear to ear. She thought it would not do any harm in having lunch. She enjoyed the attention, and not to mention, to expensive meals. She would work her subtle charm to keep the good meals coming her way, especially since; she operated on a strict budget.

"I'll call you to set up our next lunch date," Robert responded. He opened her car door for her to enter. She smiled at him and drove off. A tingling sensation tapped inside her heart like butterflies floating in a garden.

The valet driver drove up with Robert's Mercedes. He tipped the driver for both him and Tiffany. They knowingly smiled at each other as men do when one has scored a touchdown with a pretty lady.

CHAPTER 5 - THE RIGHT PRICE

Only fifteen days left before Christmas and Tiffany was anxious for the holiday shopping season to be over. The crowds annoyed her. Baby strollers were loaded with tons of shopping bags, while mothers juggled squirming babies in their arms. The teenagers, unchained from their parents' leash, roamed the malls recklessly. People who hibernated in their homes, year-round, sprang to life. She loved what Christmas represented, but the commercialism displeased her. Celebrating the birth of the Lord was joy she held dear to heart. She relished the time to enjoy family and friends.

Tiffany longed for the simple life of Sunset Bayou; life without the chaotic mess, especially during the holiday season. Her wish would come true in a couple of weeks as she was coming up on her weeklong vacation. Her small town roots still grew deep beneath the surface; however, it sometimes amazed her at how she once longed to leave the rural town, and spread her wings in the big city, only now longing to return to native soil that could nurture and revive her. The Sunset Bayou soil cultivated the seeds of her past.

As Tiffany weaved through the maze of shoppers, and memories of home paraded through her mind, Jackie strolled through the mall, wide-eyed, like a kid in a candy store. She lived to shop. Her free time revolved around canvassing boutiques, shoe stores, jewelry stores, and everything else which could adorn her from head to toe. Shopping helped fill the void that consumed her. Unlike Tiffany, she did not have any family to fly back home to; no soil where her roots were planted. Jackie's ailing grandmother, resilient to the bittersweet end, passed away not long after her college graduation. Grandma Meme hung onto the smallest ounce of strength, and every labored gasp of breath that God allowed to flow through her body, until the very end. She was determined to see her grandbaby graduate from college; the grandbaby that she raised and reared as her own, her son's only child.

Jackie pulled Tiffany by the arm, like she was a rag doll, after spotting a large red sale sign at her favorite boutique store. Like an expert navigator, she strategically weaved through the maze of shoppers.

"Girl, what are you trying to do? Rip a sister apart," Tiffany exclaimed. She dodged to her left to avoid a head collision with another frustrated shopper.

"Sale, girlfriend. You know how I am," Jackie stated excitedly. Her shoe heels clicked noisily on the gleaming floor tile as she walked faster towards the store.

"Yes, I do. You need to go easy on the spending," Tiffany scolded her best friend. She knew Jackie had a weakness for the latest trends in clothes. She also knew, too well, that Jackie often went overboard.

"I promise to buy something on sale," Jackie stated like a wife who had just been warned by her husband.

The pair walked into the boutique, one giddy like a child in a toy store, the other cautious like a soldier in a mine field. Jackie moved from rack to rack, gingerly touching the clothing which was arranged neatly on the racks. She only shopped in the exclusive, high-end stores. She admired the well-coordinated outfits that dressed up the mannequins, perfectly aligned and neatly stacked clothes on display, and the sales associates catering to her needs, which added to the splendor.

After growing up in a rural town with no fancy shopping malls, Jackie yearned to shop in the extravagant boutiques with an assortment of fine fabrics, a rainbow of colors, a variety of textures, and an array of styles. Grandma Meme sewed all of Jackie's clothes when she was a little girl. She and grandma traveled to the fabric store as a monthly routine. Grandma Meme purchased an assortment of patterns – gingham, polka dots, plaid, paisley, and floral prints. She purchased yards of cotton, taffeta, silk, and gabardine fabrics to sew a homemade designer collection of the latest patterns for Jackie's wardrobe. Jackie admired grandma's skills of weaving the finest homemade fashions, but she vowed to herself that once she lived on her own, she would never wear homemade clothes again.

Jackie relished every piece of clothing in the boutique like they would disappear at a moment's notice. Imaging the outfit she would triumph with as the ultimate prize, Jackie became oblivious to Tiffany's scolding words. She knew Tiffany did not understand her need to shop, to acquire fancy trinkets, and to adorn herself with extravagance. Some people need food, some need alcohol, some need cigarettes, and some people just need something; anything to plug up that hollow hole that resided in their hearts. Clothes did the trick for Jackie. When she looked good on the outside, she felt pretentiously good on the inside.

Jackie paired a silk turquoise blouse, splashed with colors of black and white, along with a pair of black slacks. She strode off to the dressing room with her goodies in tow.

Tiffany lingered around the sale rack and noticed that Jackie obviously overlooked it because neither piece of the trendy outfit was taken from that rack. Even the sale prices were too steep for Tiffany's frugal budget. Her small town mentality held her captive to seeking out much smaller prices. The bargain stores, with knockoff designer clothes, satisfied her taste. Right now, Tiffany only wanted to focus on her shopping list. She always saved herself for last;

putting other's needs ahead of her own.

Jackie walked out of the dressing room like a model parading on the catwalk in a couture fashion show.

"Well, what do you think?" Jackie asked with arms held out.

"It looks great. Is it on *sale*?" Tiffany asked with a scolding undertone.

"No, but it looks good," Jackie said with a sheepish grin. "And it will look perfect with my new black Stuart Weitzman sling backs." She placed her hands on her hips. Jackie, accustomed to Tiffany's motherly scolding about her excessive spending, always had a cute comeback. She knew that Tiffany's small town roots dominated her in the area of frugality. Jackie had inherited a sizeable amount of money from her parents' life insurance policies. Not to mention, Grandma Meme left her a sizeable amount of money that was stashed in the *Flour* jar; a jar that was so pretty that grandma told everybody it was for show only.

Jackie headed to the cash register with her prized outfit. She felt complete and whole while holding the silky blouse and the wool pants. The empty feeling that resided inside her heart was filled temporarily. The holiday season always brought extreme loneliness for Jackie, especially since the death of her parents. And now that Meme had passed away, the whole holiday hoopla had no meaning. For now, the holiday season was just another opportunity to find another great outfit, and another opportunity to bury the hurt, pain, and shame all of which held claim to her present.

As the girls exited the store, Tiffany could not help but to lecture Jackie about the extravagant purchase. "So, you just had to buy that outfit?"

"Look Tiff, you don't understand. The holiday season is not easy for me. I don't have any family to connect with," Jackie uttered sadly.

"Sorry, I don't mean to be hard on you, but I care about you," Tiffany stated sympathetically.

"Have you ever lost someone you loved?" Jackie asked with a distant look in her eyes. "Do you know what it's like to miss someone you love? And besides, Mama and I always shopped. It was our favorite thing to do." She tossed the shopping bag over her arm; suddenly it felt like the weight of the package increased rapidly.

"No, I haven't lost anyone," Tiffany replied. "But, there is a part of me I don't know. So, I don't know if you can miss someone you've never known." Her words were hollow and empty like an eagle's nest after all the young ones have taken their first flight of independence.

"Well, like Grandma Meme always told me, *Life is a cycle of new beginnings*. I guess we must both let go of the past and live each day as a new start."

"You're right," Tiffany said with a faint smile.

"We don't need to get all mushy in the mall anyway," Jackie stated trying to sound upbeat.

"And besides, you're my family. I love you like a sister," Tiffany remarked mimicking Jackie's pretentious upbeat attitude.

"Thanks girl. I know you mean well. I love you too. And I can't wait to go home with you to see Mama."

CHAPTER 6 - BUMPS IN THE ROAD

Tiffany and Jackie buzzed along Highway 5 heading east into the sunrise. The sun, well ahead of them, was glistening drops of gold on the tar topped road. Tiffany's black Mazda sped pass the empty scenes of the countryside. The brown cows, black horses, and patches of white sheep spotted the green pastures as motorists raced along the blacktopped highway breaking through the early morning silence.

Holiday tunes played on the radio as the duo sang karaoke style to each oldie that the DJ dusted off and rotated into spin. Tiffany brewed with anxiety to see Mama. Months had passed since her last visit home for the Fourth of July. The long, boring drive to Sunset Bayou limited her trips to holidays and emergencies only. But the simplicity of the bayou is what Tiffany longed to indulge in for this trip. The simple life eliminated confusion and brought a welcomed solitude. It was her time to fly solo and balance her external with the internal.

Since she was a child, Tiffany had always been called the all-American girl next door. She was like homemade apple pie and baseball. She tried earnestly to maintain her good girl image, at all times, as she always listened and obeyed Mama. She obediently attended church services, diligently worked in school, and selflessly volunteered in the community. Tiffany was not in search of fame or glory; she just led a good honest life.

A complete, whole family was what she most desired. Since her father never acknowledged her, or even made himself known, she knew in her heart that God was the loving Father that comforted her, guided her, and protected her. She knew, in her heart, that God would give her a complete family to love in His perfect timing.

"Girl, how much longer 'til we reach your hometown?" Jackie asked impatiently. She never enjoyed long car rides. The claustrophobic feeling of confinement in a car, for long periods, brought on painful memories of her parents' fatal car accident. Memories that were etched in her mind with a permanent marker.

The night that Sheriff Bailey knocked on Meme's door, bearing the burden of bad news, flashed through Jackie's mind. She listened while standing behind the kitchen door which was cracked just enough so that her almond shaped brown eyes could watch Meme talking with the Sheriff. Grandma wrapped one arm around her waist and the other wrinkled brown hand grasped her mouth to shield the escaping scream from her circle shaped mouth.

At the tender age of twelve years old, Jackie could barely grasp the enormity of the news that the Sheriff earnestly tried to deliver with compassion. She waited for Meme to call her into the tiny living room, remembering her manners not to meddle in grown folks' business.

After what seemed like an eternity to Jackie, grandma beckoned for her to sit on the tweed olive-green sofa covered with a pastel knitted throw. Jackie noticed the tearstained cheeks, the red streaked glassy eyes, and the trembling dark brown lips as grandma tried to regain her composure. Jackie replayed the conversation in her mind like it happened yesterday.

"Pumpkin, Grandma Meme has some sad news."

"Is it about Mama and Daddy?"

"Yes, baby."

"What is it Grandma? Is it bad news?"

"Yes, baby."

"I'm a big girl Grandma. What is it?"

"Pumpkin, Mama and Daddy were in a car accident."

"Are they in the hospital?"

"No, baby. They didn't survive the accident. Both of them were…," Grandma's voice had trailed off, unable to bring herself to say the words, *killed or dead.*

"Are they in heaven with Grandpa?" Tears started to flow down Jackie's cheeks like tiny silver streams. She wiped away the wetness with the back of her hand. She missed her mama already, and only a small part of her daddy.

"Yes, baby, in Heaven. Are you ok sweetie?"

Jackie nodded her head up and down. She finally managed to softly say, "I'm ok. Are you ok Grandma?"

An emotional part of Jackie died long before the crash that claimed the lives of her mama and daddy. Her emotional death happened in the midnight hour, in the quiet of the night. The creaking door, as it opened, broke the silence of the night and broke the bonded trust of the father and daughter relationship.

Grandma could not respond to Jackie's question nor did she have the strength to go on for the moment. She motioned for Jackie to go to her bedroom, while she took a moment to pull herself together. Jackie overheard Grandma call Addie Pearl on the telephone, the next door neighbor, who Grandma spent many long evenings rocking and talking with on the old wooden porch.

"Meet me on the porch, Addie. It's gonna be a long night. Sheriff Bailey just left with some bad news 'bout my boy, Howard, and his wife, Dorothy.

"A car accident. Jackie's still here with me. She's sleeping right now.

"I don't know how I'm gonna make it alone with a little girl. She's only twelve years old, and I'm up in age.

"Yeah, I know she can help out around the house. I don't know....I'll see you in a minute, Addie. Don't forget the coffee." That was one thing Meme could count on Addie Pearl for and that was a strong cup of chicory coffee and a good listening ear.

Addie knocked on the doorframe and a piece of alabaster colored paint chipped and fell. Meme and Addie settled heavily into the old wooden rocking chairs, perched on the front porch. The sweet smell of orange blossoms mingled with the heat's humidity that permeated the night air. The chorus of crickets created their distinctive tune and fireflies lit up the night as their light infused bodies danced back and forth.

Jackie eased her petite body to the side of the opened front door which was shielded by the wired screen door. She always had eavesdropped on Meme and Addie Pearl's gossip sessions. She listened to conservations as the two old ladies talked about everything from the economic hardship of the Walkers, the tipping out of Joe Brown on his wife, Lucille, and even the unspoken, unthinkable pregnancy of the unwed teenager, Wanda Johnson.

Tonight was different. The center of the conversation focused on Jackie. She heard her name just as she rested her peachy cheek on the doorframe careful to remain hidden in the shadows.

"Here's your coffee," Addie stated matter-of-factly. Her years on this earth had created a steel shield around her, which protected her from happiness and hurt. Not much of anything created a stir or an emotional response from Addie. She was like an anchor that steadied the ship docked in the harbor.

"Thank you sweetie." Meme grabbed the hot cup of coffee and wrapped both hands around the cup. "Oh, Addie...what now? First, Felix done died on me...now Howard and Dorothy. What I'm gonna do? Especially with a twelve year old." Meme rocked back and forth.

"I know it's hard," Addie stated scratching her silver wiry locks with a fingernail yellowed by time and age. Days of shelling peas, snapping green beans, and shucking corn wrinkled her once soft and supple honey colored hands. Her hands were wrinkled from countless days of washing and scrubbing with lye soap that caused more harm than good.

"I'm way up in years. My childrearing days are long gone. I love my grandbaby and want what's best for her, but I'm tired. She'll become a young woman soon. You know what I mean. Lil boys, and the birds and bees talk…" Meme stared out in the darkness of the night. Her eyes were hallowed and empty.

"Take it one day at time." Addie reassured her best friend.

"One day at time…that's what I'm trying to do. Every time I think I can move on ahead in life, the Lord puts another stumbling block in my way." The cup of chicory coffee warmed Meme's hands, but not her soul. She remained troubled with worry and uncertainty, but she knew that she had to hold up and stay strong for Jackie.

"You know the Lord loves you and he will never leave you nor forsake you. You just have to trust him. And besides, Jackie is a good child. She'll help you 'round the house; and you know you need the help. Sometimes the Lord sends us blessings in disguise, but we brush'em off cause it's not what we want or what we understand." Addie waved her hand in the air mimicking the motion of throwing away the blessing.

"You right Addie. I do need some help with cleaning and running errands. She young and smart. I just hope we both can cope and deal with the loss. I know life is a cycle of new beginnings. I just have to focus on the Lord and his goodness. He always brings us through the storm." Meme released a soft sigh of relief.

"Oh Addie. Thank you for always being here. You a good friend. Always listening and never judging." Meme rocked back and forth in the old wooden chair with the chipped red paint. Felix gave it to Meme as a birthday present when her age turned to the half-century mark. She rocked, keeping the time with the musical chirps of the crickets. With each rocking movement, she rubbed her frail fingers up and down her cushy brown arms as they rested across her bosom.

Jackie withdrew from eavesdropping to return to her bed careful to avoid the creaky wooden boards. She did not want to draw attention to the fact that she had been listening to grown folks conversation. She understood some of Meme's worries. Her young mind still was incapable of fully grasping the idea of how their lives had changed in a split second. However, she was determined not to be a burden for Meme. She would do her chores as instructed. She would not complain about Meme sewing her dresses on the old black Singer sewing machine. She crawled into her twin-sized bed and covered up with Meme's prized homemade quilt.

Jackie was jolted back to the present as Tiffany slowed down to exit at Harry's Rest Stop. The girls marched into the roadside store and purchased chips and sodas, as appetizers, to curve their hunger pains until they reached Tiffany's hometown.

"So, what's the answer to my question…How much longer?" Traveling along the same highway that her parents' drove for the last time had Jackie sitting on pins and needles.

"We haven't even reached the state line yet." Tiffany responded with a sly grin on her face.

"I guess I should put on my patient pants."

"Yeah, enjoy the scenery," Tiffany said jokingly.

"Scenery. Right. Girlfriend, cows and horses are not scenery," Jackie remarked with a hint of sarcasm.

"Well, we have about three more hours," Tiffany stated as she eased the car back onto the highway to continue their trip into the morning sun.

"Ok," Jackie sighed. "What is Mama cooking?" Jackie had adopted Ms. Luella as her play mom, since her parents were deceased and Grandma Meme had passed. She didn't have any other family to bond with or to love.

"All the good stuff - fried turkey, cornbread dressing, dirty rice, and to top it all off, sweet potato pie," Tiffany exclaimed with the juices flowing in her mouth just thinking about the delicious feast.

"Umm, I can feel the pounds packing on right now, but I'm not complaining," Jackie said excitedly. She always prepared for Ms. Luella's home cooking by adding in an extra workout.

"Anything new with your *new* man, Kevin?" Tiffany asked.

"He is awesome, girl. We had dinner at the new Italian restaurant, Emilo's," Jackie stated with an air of just falling in love.

"Oh, nice. What's he like? After all, I am living vicariously through your love life."

"Come on, Tiff. You'll find somebody," Jackie said with sympathy. She understood Tiffany's loneliness and her desire to find a suitable mate to fill in the hollow hole that swelled and consumed the essence of her soul.

"How about the man you met? Have you heard from him?" Jackie asked.

"Girl, he sent me pink roses and signed the card as a secret admirer. Had me going for a moment, then he called." Tiffany did not want to confess that she was warming up to idea of the possibility of a romance with this man.

"What did he have to say?" Jackie munched on a bag of potato chips to help curve the hunger pains.

"He asked me to go to lunch." Tiffany replied nonchalantly.

"Well, are you going to go?"

"Yes." Tiffany responded quickly and to the point.

"That's all you have to say is…Yes. Details please. Where are you going and when? You were all up in *my* business."

"We went to Chez Gumbeaux's. It was very nice. He's sweet. But it was just lunch so don't staring thinking anything else," Tiffany said nonchalantly. She did not want make more out of the date than what she wanted. She did not want to build herself up only to be disappointed once again.

"What happened? I want all the details," Jackie asked excitedly. She wiggled in her seat waiting for Tiffany to recount every detail.

"He is an oil and gas business executive, so he is very professional. He has a clean cut, polished look, and great taste. He wears an Armani suit very well. He is six feet and has skin smooth like maple. He is a little pudgy, but maybe, eventually, we can work out at the gym together and whip that body into shape. I didn't see any signs of a wedding band. You know that is rule number one…inspect for the evidence. So in the end, it was a very good first date."

"First date…is that an indication that there will be more dates?"

"Maybe, but let me finish with the details. After all, you did ask. The conversation was interesting and funny. He told me that I remind him of someone he once knew. And I told him I'm an original and there isn't a duplicate. It is obvious that he's been broken in, 'cause he definitely knows how to treat a lady." Tiffany let a smile creep across her face.

"That's great Tiff."

The girls continued to ride along the near empty highway while chatting, giggling, and singing every song that blasted on the radio.

"Did you feel a thump? What's that noise?" Jackie asked nervously.

"Oh, no sounds like the back tire," Tiffany remarked with concern. She eased her foot off the gas pedal and coasted to the shoulder of the highway. There was not another gas station, or car repair shop, for miles. She couldn't believe this was happening. The tires were only a year old. Mama would worry about their location since she knew exactly how long the drive was from Dallas to Sunset. Five hours and forty-five minutes, if Tiffany drove the speed limit; however, that was on a rare occasion. The girls went to work hoisting up the car, unbolting the nuts on the tire, rolling the battered tire to the trunk, and rolling out the pintsized replacement. Almost an hour had passed before the makeshift mechanics were coasting again down Highway 5.

CHAPTER 7 - OLDIES BUT GOODIES

Luella relished her tiny three bedroom home, passed down to her from her mother. Property always remained in the family. That was the way it was done in the south, especially on the bayou. The prized plot of land, at 416 Washington Avenue, was a treasure to keep and pass down from generation to generation. The little house showed its marks of time -- a slight lean to the right, the cracked sidewalk, and the gravely driveway.

Luella did her best to upgrade and upkeep her precious home, precious in her eyes at least. Just last summer, she hired the Mayo brothers to paint the bungalow a fresh apricot with a clean linen trim. The tattered wooden rocking chair rested easy on the front porch. The old Magnolia tree still stood firm in the front yard withstanding the test of time and weathering the worst of storms.

Christmas classics, oldies but goodies, played in the background and kept Luella feeling lively and energetic. She danced from room to room, dusting and vacuuming. She cleaned every crack and corner for a fresh, new smell when her baby girl, Tiffany, arrived with her adopted baby girl, Jackie.

Luella put freshly washed sheets on the twin beds in Tiffany's room. The flowers, that decorated the sheets, were like a vibrant spring garden which coordinated perfectly with the lavender comforter set. She even decorated an imitation table-top Christmas tree with miniature ornaments and twinkling lights, for Tiffany's dresser, so that the holiday spirit permeated throughout the house.

Now that the cleaning was done, Luella shifted her dance steps to the kitchen. The turkey lay seasoned in the roaster, the rice was washed and ready for the boiling pot, the eggs rested in the mixing bowls, and the butter softened, as it sat on the tan speckled countertop. Luella collected and assembled her cooking utensils -- the measuring cup and spoons, the ceramic mixing bowls, the worn baking pans, and the holiday decorated oven mitts. All were arranged in their appropriate sections and positions for the dish they would prepare. Luella viewed cooking as an art. The palette of ingredients had to be prepped. The oven had to be heated to the perfect temperature. She missed working at Petre's Café. Cooking was close to her heart. She tried to come up with the money to buy the café, after Petre's death, but the bank's price was too high and she did not like the new owner. So she moved on to other things; not necessarily better, just different.

Luella measured the rice for the steaming pot. Dirty rice was her baby girl's favorite dish. Luella's mind drifted back in time remembering that Tiffany's father's favorite food was dirty rice also. Tiffany favored her father in more ways than one. He always dropped by Petre's for a bowl of dirty rice, good conversation, and to enjoy the view, Luella that is. One quiet Thursday, he dropped by, later than his usual lunchtime, only a couple of hours before closing. His hearing at the courthouse ran late, so he decided to drop by Petre's before heading home. Luella sashayed over to the corner booth.

"Jack, what are you doing in here this late?" She eyed him while flashing a devilish smile.

"Hearing ran late. The Judge wanted everything in order today." Jack loosened his necktie, unbuttoned his shirt cuffs and rolled his sleeves midway up his arms.

"You're a hardworking man," Luella said. She gazed sensuously into his pale blue eyes.

"Yes ma'am, I am." Jack stared into her hazelnut eyes. He wrapped his hands around the coffee cup and stroked the cup gently.

"No need to be formal with me. You know we're like old friends." She stood erect with an arch in her back rounded like a bow waiting for the arrow to be fired. She tapped her fingertips on the table just inches from where Jack held onto his coffee mug.

"Of course, we're like old friends. I've always admired you, Luella," Jack stated flashing a shiny grin and toying with his necktie.

"Don't get mushy on me, now," Luella said with a sweet, sly smile as she turned to walk toward the speckled white countertop to give Petre his usual order. Luella glanced over her shoulder and noticed Jack watching her walk away. His eyes were glassy and distant and his lips were moist. He touched the corner of his pink lips to wipe away the wetness.

Luella snapped back to the present when she heard two car doors slam. She tucked away her memories of Jack. She did not need those memories anymore. Tiffany was a constant reminder of their love. She hurried to the front door and there was her baby girl looking pretty as always.

Tiffany and Jackie walked up the cracked sidewalk grinning from ear to ear. Tiffany was happy to see Mama's smiling face, while Jackie was happy to be released from the confines of the car.

Luella welcomed the girls with hugs and kisses. The aroma of the home cooking wafted throughout the house and up to the front door, and welcomed the duo into the warmth and coziness of the bungalow.

"Oh, Mama, it smells good up in here." Tiffany hugged Luella tightly and kissed her gently on the cheek. "And your cheeks are rosy. What's up with you?"

"You know I always have something good for my baby. And I'm just excited to see my baby." Luella hugged her back. She prohibited herself to speak about Tiffany's father, especially with her daughter. She wanted life to remain uncomplicated, without explanations. Each time Tiffany would ask her about the details of her father, she conveniently changed the subject. As the years passed, Tiffany stopped asking, which provided welcomed relief for Luella. She did not want to lie to her baby girl, but she did not want to face the truth either.

She then stepped back to look over Tiffany from head to toe. She examined Tiffany to determine how much fattening up she would need while home for the holidays.

"We are starving Ms. Luella," Jackie stated while unbuttoning her denim jacket.

"I'm sure you are. What took ya'll so long?" Luella asked with a quizzical look on her round, dewy face. Her complexion was smooth and creamy like milk. The rust-colored ribbed sweater and denim jeans showed off her bowling pin figure that she still maintained.

"We had a flat tire," Tiffany stated.

"Well, everything is ok, now. Isn't it?" Luella asked with concern in her eyes.

"Yes ma'am. Tiffany sure does know how to handle an axle," Jackie remarked with a lighthearted grin.

"Baby, when there isn't a man around the house, you have to learn how to be independent. And besides, I didn't raise my daughter to be dependent on anyone," Luella proudly stated draping her arm around Tiffany's shoulders.

"Come into the kitchen and I'll fix ya'll some lunch." They marched into the tiny kitchen. The girls sat giggling at the square table while Luella heaped mounds of food on their plates.

The entire week was filled with food, laughter, and love. The girls enjoyed listening to Luella talk about the good old days when life seemed to be carefree and everybody was happy. Even though Jackie could feel the love that radiated from Tiffany and Ms. Luella, she still longed for the feeling of Meme's warm, soft hands and her parents' hugs and kisses. The emptiness that resided in Jackie's heart only occupied half the space. The warmth of the Guillory's helped to occupy the other half.

CHAPTER 8 - SWEET SURPRISES

The shiny black sports car spun into the garage beneath Jackie's downtown apartment building on 7777 Main Street. An historic landmark, refurbished into trendy urban lofts, offered Jackie the lifestyle she had always desired. With his sports car parked diagonally harboring two parking spaces, Kevin grabbed the spring bouquet of purple irises, yellow daffodils, fuchsia Gerber daisy, and sprigs of baby's breath, and raced to the elevator. He was already thirty minutes late. He knew Jackie would cut him a look sharp enough to cut through a block of ice. Kevin rang the bell and plastered on his dazzling smile, mentally preparing his defense for his repeated tardiness. Jackie opened the door with an exasperated look and let out a deep sigh.

"Sorry, babe," Kevin mouthed. His face contorted with his bottom lip sagging low and his eyes drooped like a puppy dog.

"Don't give me that pitiful played out look. It's not going to work," Jackie said determined not to fall for the pathetic look.

Kevin swung his arm around from behind his back with the colorful flowers hoping his backup defense would warm the chilly reception. A small grin slowly crept its way onto Jackie's face; however she quickly dismissed it. Her patience was paper thin with his repeated tardiness and lame excuses. She had already let him slip past her three-strikes and you are out rule. She felt he was the one, the man she prayed about, the man she conjured up in every daydream. "You know the show started fifteen minutes ago!"

"Babe, I know. I tried to get here on time, but…" Kevin walked behind Jackie posed with a pathetic slumped over demeanor.

"But, nothing. We have this same discussion every time. I've had enough…" Jackie walked away from him, not wanting to hear another excuse.

"Don't throw me to the curb sweetie." Kevin reached out to grab her arm.

"Throw you! I'm going to kick you…" She jerked back away from him.

Kevin finally managed to quickly pull her to him and locked his sweet lips to hers before she could mouth, or even think, another word. She hesitantly pulled away from the luscious lips which were locked to hers and sent magnetic, electric pulses up and down her spine. She stared into his blazing brown eyes which melted the ice enveloped around her heart.

"Can you please try to be on time, the next time?" Jackie pleaded.

"Of course sweetie, anything for you. Let's go. We'll just go to dinner and then I have a surprise for you later."

"Surprise, umm hmm. What do you have in mind?" Kevin had showed her how much he cared about her with several little surprises since they started dating. He showered her with flowers delivered to her office, romantic dinners at the most expensive restaurants, candlelit bubble baths after a strenuous day, and her favorite of all, a picnic in the park.

Jackie and Kevin walked hand-in-hand through downtown Dallas. They walked to Sorrento, the jazz café located a couple of blocks from Jackie's apartment. The warm night air, coupled with Kevin's gentle touches, caressed Jackie's skin and helped her to relax and enjoy the evening. She did not have the ability or the desire to remain angry with him for long. She wanted to maintain the peace at all cost. The relationship felt like Heaven. Everything floated along carefree like the fluffy clouds that drifted in the sky. Not to mention, Kevin's carefree personality always made her feel lighthearted.

After the hostess seated the couple in a secluded corner, Jackie could not stand the suspense any longer.

"What's the surprise?" Jackie asked like a kid on Christmas morning eager to know what is in the gift box.

"Can't wait can you?" Kevin sipped on his drink to avoid answering her. He wanted to keep building up the suspense.

"Of course not. You want me to be patient."

"I know how hard you've been working on the Anissá clothing line account. Here is an opportunity for you to take some time and relax," Kevin mouthed casually as he handed her a small envelope. Jackie thought *an envelope…what can be in an envelope. I want a small box.*

"Sweetie, a gift card to the Serenity Spa! I love you!" Jackie yelped as she pulled the contents from the envelope. She contained her disappointment that the package was not what she hoped for.

"I love you too. Anything for my baby. And it also marks the three months since we started dating."

"Oh, Kevin, you remembered. I always knew there was something special about you from the first time I saw." Jackie knew she would have to wait a little longer to acquire her prized possession, the engagement ring.

"Of course you knew. How couldn't you. I'm a great guy!" Kevin stated with his usual arrogance.

"And still puffed up with pride. I guess your self-confidence is somewhat attractive also. But don't overdo it or I'll drop you like a bad habit"

"Hey, be nice to a brotha. I'm the man of your dreams." Kevin smiled. He knew there had been many of times when women told him that he was the man of their dreams.

"Maybe or maybe not. Don't get too comfortable, brotha."

"You know there is a connection between us. And there is no sense in denying it. The first time I saw you, I thought to myself *there is a classy, sexy lady.*"

"Of course you did. You know quality when you see it."

After dinner, they headed back to Jackie's apartment instead of searching for additional entertainment to fill the evening. The bright lights of the downtown skyline lit the path back to Jackie's apartment. The duo stopped periodically to tenderly kiss and gaze into each other's eyes. The electricity was running rampantly. Quick, hot flashes pulsated throughout Jackie's veins. She wanted tonight to be the night that she and Kevin made love. The evening started out shaky, in a bad way, but she hoped that it ended shaky in a good way.

As soon as the doors to the elevator in Jackie's apartment building closed, the two grabbed each other, wrapped their arms around the other, and embraced in a deep passionate kiss. The ride up in the elevator was intense, magnetic, and steamy. Jackie fumbled around in her purse searching for her keys to unlock the front door, as Kevin pushed up on her from behind and resting his warm hands on the curve of her hips. She felt his manhood piercing through his slacks, ready for some serious lovemaking.

She could not focus on inserting the key into the front door for feeling the heat from his body and the throbbing sensation in her now moist black lace panties. She finally forced the door open and two fell into the living room holding on to each other for dear life. Jackie guided Kevin to her bedroom. He touched her lips with his fingers and she graciously opened her mouth to invite one finger in at time. The scent of his spicy cologne drifted up into Jackie's nostrils causing her to feel a dizzying sensation. He caressed her plump, round breast with one hand while picking away the lacy black bra with the other one. She grabbed him by the waist and pulled him closer to her. She placed one hand on his bare back and the other hand on his hard derriere. They undressed each other, slowly and seductively, in between kisses and caresses.

The night was long with passionate lovemaking. Jackie lightly rubbed the perspiration from Kevin's brow after he reached his climatic moment. They kissed and drifted off to sleep still holding on to each other.

The brightness of the sun replaced the glow of the moonlight as dawn began to break. Her apartment was nestled on the eighteenth floor. There was no need for blinds or draperies. She loved the huge picture window that overlooked the postcard picture of downtown.

Jackie woke to the savory smell of bacon and eggs. She thought she was dreaming. She reached over to feel for Kevin and only discovered rumpled sheets. Just as she was about to climb out of the bed, the door opened and Kevin stood there framed like a chiseled Greek god. He held a tray of breakfast goodies; an omelet, crisp bacon, and orange juice. Jackie smiled.

"What have you been up to?"

"After last night's workout, I know my baby is hungry," Kevin stated flashing his sexy smile. Jackie blushed coyly.

"You filled me up with the taste of your sexy chocolate."

"I've awakened the tiger in you."

"You made all the right moves, sweetie…from the head to the toes."

"You like the magic I worked on your toes, pumpkin?"

"Ummm hmmm. Baby you were off the chain," Jackie stated while diving her fork into the omelet. "This is delicious, darling. A man who can cook in the kitchen and in the bedroom," Jackie stated with a sly, sexy smile plastered on her face.

The smile that Kevin put on Jackie's face was not only from their passionate lovemaking, but from the fact that she was able to open her heart to him. She trusted him. He was always there when she needed someone to talk to. He was that someone who provided solid advice and was a rock in the times of distress. She sensed, and now experienced, that he knew how to treat a woman. His mama taught him well. He did not know his father nor did he want to know him. He vowed to himself to always treat a woman special, and with dignity, just like his mama showed him.

Kevin noticed the colorful handmade quilt gracefully displayed on Jackie's bedroom wall. He put on his boxer shorts and walked to the corner to admire the cherished work of art.

"Hey sweetheart, where did you get the quilt?" Kevin gently touched the quilt with his hand.

"My grandma Meme made it for my dad, and when he passed away, she gave it to me."

"Wow, it is beautiful. Grandma had talent." He continued to admire the handiwork of Jackie's grandmother. His grandmother passed away before he was born. His family was small, just his mom, baby brother and himself. His mom instilled him the real values of how to treat a lady.

"She loved to sew. She made all of my clothes." Jackie sat on the edge of the bed wrapped in her robe.

"That's why you have such a keen eye for fashion."

"I guess that is one way of putting it. I wasn't too fond of the homemade stuff."

"What about your parents? You never talk about them." Kevin stated hoping she would continue to open up. She never offered much detail about her life history. The book was closed and on the shelf, not available for checking out.

"There isn't much to tell and it's very difficult to talk about. They were killed in a car crash when I was twelve years old," Jackie said evasively. She avoided the topic of her parents' death like the plague. The memories were unbearable. Jackie envisioned her parents' metallic silver 1981 Cadillac, but her mind did not allow her to picture her parents' bodies, mangled and lifeless lying along the roadside. She suppressed the images of their bodies as far back into the crevices of her mind until it was smaller than a pea. A lot of memories, especially unpleasant memories, were shoved into the far corners of Jackie's mind throughout the years. Her mind had become like rows of gravesites; each memory buried six feet under was marked 'Do Not Disturb'. Her memories had spiraled down into the depths of her soul and only as time progressed would they slowly surface.

"Well, don't you have something to do today? I know it is Saturday, but any errands to run or go to the gym?" Jackie asked bluntly.

"Yeah, I have a couple of things I can get into," Kevin stated looking confused at Jackie. *Why the big rush to get rid of him? Was she having second thoughts about last night?* He thought to himself. He was not accustomed to women rushing him or brushing him off. His persona always demanded attention and respect.

"Are you pushing a brotha off?" Kevin walked to where Jackie sat on the bed and sat beside her.

"No, it's not like that sweetie. I can be with you always, but I have to go to the office today for a few hours," Jackie replied. Work was always her excuse for dodging the difficult subject about her parents.

"Ms. Workaholic," Kevin stated after planting a juicy wet kiss on Jackie's forehead. "I'll call you later, pumpkin."

Pumpkin, the nickname Meme had given her at birth; her little pumpkin.

Chapter 9 – Memory Lane

After Kevin left, Jackie wrapped herself in her cozy cranberry colored terry cloth bathrobe and padded softly across the floor, of her bedroom, over to the quilt that hung neatly on a steel rod in the corner. The morning sunlight splashed a bright light through the picture window onto the quilt illuminating the lively colored patterns. She gently traced the irregular shaped shades of deep violet, ruddy red, earthy brown, sunny yellow, and grassy green all stitched together to form one large perfect rectangle.

The gently worn quilt covered Jackie's mind with the warmness of good memories and the discomfort of bad memories from long ago. The conflicting emotions, that surfaced, created a bittersweet uneasiness. A part of Jackie wanted to discard the quilt when she thought about who the original owner was, but another part of her wanted to cling to the loving memories of Meme since it was her gentle hands that delicately stitched each piece of fabric into its permanent position.

Caressing the quilt, Jackie was transported back in time to the place when her nightmares first flared up. They harassed her constantly. Meme did everything to ease her grandbaby's mind. She fixed warm milk, sang soft songs, and even, at times, let Jackie share her bed. But this night, she remembered how Meme nestled Jackie in her warm, chocolate arms. She spoke just above a whisper to calm Jackie, once again, after another terrifying nightmare. Ever since Jackie moved in with Grandma Meme, after her parents' fatal car crash, the nightmares became constant. Jackie could never bring herself to describe the nightmares to Meme. She could not speak the unbearable truth.

"Are you dreaming about your parents, sweetheart?" Meme asked as she squeezed Jackie in her arms.

"Yes, ma'am," Jackie stated. She rested her head in Meme's bosom.

"I know you miss your mama and daddy. But you know my 'lil pumpkin, life is like an endless cycle of new beginnings. A lesson I learned when your grandpa passed away a few years ago. I did not know how I was going to go on living and making ends meet. Each day I had to push away the fears of being alone. After fifty-two years of marriage, you settle into one being, an inseparable person, thoughts intertwined, finishing each other's sentences."

Jackie sat quietly and enjoyed the soothing comfort of Meme's voice. She always liked when Meme talked about the good old days, remembering the happy times with Grandpa. The happy memories allowed Jackie to sense a small of morsel of peace.

"Baby girl when you came to live permanently with Meme, that's when I saw a new beginning. My spirit came alive, even though the circumstances surrounding your arrival were dismal. I saw this as God's way of saying to move on, move forward with life, and that it was time for something new. God granted me the gift of a new beginning. His promises always ring true, 'I'll never leave you nor forsake you.'"

"Grandma Meme, I'll never leave you either," Jackie said with an undying affection as she wrapped her arms around Meme's neck.

"I know pumpkin. And I'll never leave you," Grandma Meme said before planting a quick, tender kiss on Jackie's forehead with her dark brown wrinkled lips. She tucked Jackie in tightly under the quilt that she had stitched with her creased brown hands for her son, Jackie's father, when he was a little boy.

Jackie dropped down heavily to sit cross-legged on the oval lamb's wool rug that lay spread out across the wooden floor. She leaned her body, wrapped in her fluffy purple robe, forward exhausted after carrying around the dead weight of bad memories that resided in her. She wanted to excavate the weight of shame and sorrow, but it seemed easier to keep the pain and memories buried. Jackie knew it was easier to immerse herself into the activities that brought pleasure instead pain. She gravitated back and forth between the desired pleasure of a perfect present and the painstaking memories of the past.

She lifted the lid of the mahogany chest, a graduation present from Meme. The hinges creaked. The lavender scent of the sachet wafted up to Jackie's nose. She shifted the pictures, trophies, dried flowers, and all the treasures she had collected throughout the years until she located her colored pencils at the bottom of the hope chest. Her fingertips finally touched and traced the edges of the tattered box. She pulled the colorful box out gingerly. The pencils were perfectly lined up, arranged in the sequence of the color of the rainbow. The vibrant colors of the pencils opened Jackie's imagination and transported her to a happier place. Happy memories flooded Jackie's mind of the day Meme brought home the colorful box of pencils purchased from Jack's Five & Dime corner store. It was no special day.

After the death of her parents, she withdrew from everything and everyone. Verbal communication was few and far between; like water being absent in a desert. The only release she allowed herself to experience was through drawing. Meme noticed Jackie's talent right off. She dipped into the cookie jar money to buy Jackie a new set of colored pencils that represented every color of the rainbow.

Those pencils inspired Jackie to become fond of drawing and art. Meme noticed Jackie's natural ability to capture the beauty of an object transposed onto paper. She enrolled Jackie in summer art classes at the local YMCA. The classes were a breakthrough. She had the opportunity to express the anger, rage, bitterness, and shame – without saying a word nor without hurting anyone the way she was hurting.

Jackie sifted through the stacks of yellowed paper until she found a blank page. She traced a large, blue circle on a piece of the drawing paper; blue – bold and beautiful, yet melancholy. Conflicting like the emotions that resided in Jackie's heart. The blue circle kept going and going. Sometimes the strokes were light and feathery, and sometimes they were hard and rough, but one end always met the other. She felt like her life was going in circles. She always ended up back at the place where she started and that was somewhere in the past.

Life is a cycle of new beginnings.

Jackie showered and dressed. Even though it was Saturday, being the overachiever that she was, going to the office was the breath of fresh air which she needed. The deadline for the Anissá account was fast approaching like a speeding bullet. She had not made any significant developments on the project and she knew significant updates were needed for the presentation to Mr. Bell at their next monthly status meeting.

Jackie pounded the pavement keeping her eyes focused on the concrete and the destination that lay ahead of her. She avoided looking to her left or to her right, avoiding her reflection in the mirrored glass steel buildings. She focused straight ahead to help ease the strain of thinking about what was behind her.

She phoned Kevin as she walked the five long blocks to her office. She knew she had to explain her contradictory behavior, but how could she. The mood swings did not make any sense to her either. One minute, happy loving feelings resonated, and the next minute, depressing feelings overwhelmed her.

"Hi sweetie. It's me," Jackie stated with a forced smile. Her feet pounded the pavement heavy like a lead anchor. She avoided looking to her left or right wanting to avoid her reflection in the shiny glass buildings.

"What's up?" Kevin asked nonchalantly. After the brush off from Jackie earlier that morning, he suited up in his red-colored basketball gear and headed to the gym. He needed to blow off the steam that had built up. He knew shooting some hoops was just the activity he needed.

"I'm sorry for acting crazy this morning," Jackie said with the sweetness of honey in her voice. She wrapped the cashmere cranberry-colored scarf around her neck to shield away the crisp, cool breeze that blew around the downtown skyscrapers.

"I hear you. Did I do anything wrong? One minute you are hot to trot, and the next you are cold as ice."

"No darling. You didn't do anything wrong. I just have a lot on my mind. This big project has me stressed me out. I'm on my way to the office right now." She was not ready to confide to Kevin about her hurtful past. Thinking about it was difficult enough and she could not image talking about it, especially with the man she loved. And even though, she trusted him, she was not ready to trust him with that deep, dark secret. What would he think of her? Would he understand? Would he run away and leave her? It was a chance she did not want to take and one she vowed not to take.

"I understand work pressure. But I'm here to help you handle that pressure in a loving way. Maybe later we can hook up and I'll show you what I mean," Kevin stated with a lovingly sly smile on his face. Kevin wanted the relationship to work with Jackie but he was only willing to give her some many chances for their relationship to survive.

"Well, aren't you the Mr. Loverman. I'll call you when I leave the office." Jackie smiled a sigh of relief.

The sky was painted a baby blue and dotted with fluffy clouds. A light breeze tap danced across the tips of trees in full bloom. A rainbow of flowers lined their path filling the air with the sweet smell of gardenia, honeysuckle, and jasmine. Tiffany and Robert strolled through Fritz Park until they found a cozy location to enjoy their afternoon picnic.

Robert had a rare Saturday afternoon available for the two of them to enjoy a romantic date, a break from their usual Thursday lunch date. Tiffany surprised at his proposal jumped at the opportunity to enjoy a romantic afternoon. She did not question his sudden availability, but happily accepted his invitation. During the course of their phone conversations and lunch dates, she had grown fond of him. She laughed at his corny jokes and listened attentively at his boring renditions about business deals. His pudginess diminished in her eyes, and his age soon became a plus, since he always offered her tidbits of wisdom.

As they walked up to the picnic table, Robert placed his plump hand in the small of Tiffany's back. His large hand nearly encircled the entire width of her tiny waist. They sat beside each other on the wooden bench. Tiffany opened the picnic basket and spread out the red and white checkered table cloth. She gingerly placed a plate in front of each of them and unpacked the sandwiches that she had hastily made.

Robert sat sidesaddle on the bench. He whispered in her ear, "I don't need any food to eat. I'll just nibble on your ear, your neck, and your lips." Tiffany blushed and continued to unpack their lunch.

He stroked the small of her back and traced the tiny flowers that adorned her sundress. She gently touched his other hand and turned to look into his eyes that sparkled with a hint of lust. "Well, I'm going to eat the food that is on our plates." She smiled and then gave him a quick kiss. His full, soft lips nearly swallowed her thin, pale lips. His hand moved from the small of her back to the nape of her neck. He twirled a lock of her hair around his finger.

"Lunch does look delicious. And I know if you made it, then

it is tasty." Robert bit a piece of his sandwich.

"Thank you darling," Tiffany responded with an air of confidence.

"How is work? Are you still stressed you out? You know I'm always willing to help relieve any kind of stress," Robert commented as she caressed her shoulders.

Tiffany tried to ignore his last comment. He did have a special way to help her forget about work and any other issues that haunted her.

"The Promise Keepers luncheon is fast approaching, so I'm working on the major details and minor details. Everything appears to be falling into place. I have to do best on this project, since my boss has a major stake in the success of this luncheon." Robert coughed like someone had swallowed too much black pepper. He did not think he would here that name from Tiffany.

"What are you working on for the Promise Keepers? Is that the name you said?" Robert asked with intense curiosity.

"Yes, and it's their annual fundraising luncheon. I'm the lead event planner on the project. My boss thought it would be a good fit for me. She really likes my work."

Robert continued chewing on his sandwich, even though, he had suddenly lost his appetite. He alternately tugged on the collar of his pale yellow Polo shirt. He rubbed away the imaginary perspiration from his brow. He wiped his palms on his khaki slacks. Tiffany continued talking about the plans for the luncheon, oblivious to his uneasiness.

"I'll have to schedule a meeting with the head of the organization and the mistress of ceremonies. There are some many things to discuss – order of the program, the meal selection, the music, the program, and the list goes on. My head is spinning like in a whirlwind. If I do well on this project, a big promotion could be coming my way. Isn't that great, sweetie?" Tiffany asked while wrapping her arms around Robert's neck. He squeezed her close to him to feel the warmth of her body as well as to hide his distressed facial expression.

"Yes, sweetie that is great," he managed to mouth out. He buried his face into her soft golden, brown hair.

Chapter 10 - Strolling the Street

Summer arrived with a blazing heat. The temperature broke records with days of 100 degree weather. Jackie whizzed along the highway in her cherry red Honda Accord, with the air conditioner blasting icy cold air, during the early Friday morning rush hour traffic to the airport, listening to KFVN news radio. She absorbed every headline and storyline.

This weekend's excursion with the girls would allow her time to relax and a chance to focus on fun. The trip would also allow her time away from Kevin. Lately his attitude had shifted into neutral from lover-man to spaceman. He needed his space, he needed time to think, and he needed *things* that did not include her.

Driving through DFW international airport was like navigating a labyrinth; always going in circles and never really going anywhere. She finally landed in the North Shuttle parking lot. She grabbed her luggage, hopped on the shuttle bus, and arrived at Terminal A. The tension of the relationship, the drive for perfection, and the haunting nightmares that kept Jackie wound up tightly, all receded like flood waters flowing into a drain. While feeling through her emotions, Jackie suddenly noticed her girlfriends at the gate to check-in. The ladies were light with laughter and ready to kick off a weekend of celebration. Jackie's friend, Alicia Hartman, was on her way to marital bliss. The weekend-long party signified her last rite of passage as a single woman.

The six ladies prepared to board the plane, ready for an excursion that was destined to create fireworks and not the kind that burst in midair. The soiree would erupt like a volcano and add hotter temperatures, than anticipated, to the fun, festive weekend.

Jackie knew all of the ladies except one and she did not seem to connect with the usual clique. She questioned why Alicia invited her to the weekend bachelorette party. After all, Alicia had only casually mentioned that she worked in the same department and that they had lunch a couple of times.

Jackie observed the woman, noticing that she was not as polished and professional like the rest of them. But, she dismissed her prejudices and packed away her biases. She did not want anything or anyone to disrupt her temporary moment of joy.

As customary, the group exchanged animated hellos and sisterly hugs. Alicia introduced her coworker to the rest of the gang.

"Ladies, I want to introduce my assistant, Theresa," Alicia stated with an attitude worthy of a diva. A chorus of '*hellos and how are you*' and rattling of names filled the air to welcome Theresa into the clique. "She has to deal with me every day and we know that isn't an easy task. So, I wanted Theresa to join us and see that I'm not all about work. And, I also wanted her to meet my wonderful friends." The ladies encircled Theresa welcoming her into the group.

The six ladies arrived at the New Orleans airport, fired up and feeling feisty. The humidity rose up and steamed their faces for an instant, free facial. Moisture sank into their perfectly coiffed hairdos to undo any shape or form of curl. Jackie thought *I should have opted for the sister girl ponytail.* She noticed that Tiffany's hair fell right into a naturally curly pattern. After all, Tiffany was a bayou girl.

The shuttle ride to the heart of the French Quarters was like riding in a space car from the Jetson's. The shuttle driver bobbed and weaved speeding along Interstate 10 like they were the only car left on the planet. Jackie prayed a quick prayer, *Lord let us make it to our hotel safely and not die in the hands of this mad-driving maniac.* God answered her prayer and the group arrived at the hotel with all body parts intact and their hearts recovered to their rightful places.

The ladies sashayed to the front desk to check-in, at the refurbished hotel in the Warehouse District, each toting overstuffed suitcases crammed with enough clothes for a week's stay. The lobby was adorned with colorful, contemporary artwork mingled with relics of history. The upholstered chairs and lounging sofa added softness with warm shades of daisy yellow, olive green, and tea-colored brown. The hardwood floors added old world charm along with the French doors and the intricate iron railing that outlined the stairs. The charm of the hotel embraced the visiting group with a relaxing atmosphere. It was just the ambience needed to kick off the celebration.

After settling into their rooms, the girls walked to the French Quarters for lunch. Each one voiced her preference. The only thing that each one had in common was the desire to indulge in some spicy Creole cooking. Tiffany, the expert on the area and the cuisine, guided the group in the right direction. She knew all the hot spots in the area where they could feast on fresh seafood, zesty jambalaya, and spicy etouffeé. But it was Alicia's weekend, so her choice won out. The ladies strolled over to Poirier's on Decatur Street. The sassy jazz greeted them at the door. The warm mahogany wood structure embraced them with old world charm.

"This weekend is going to be the bomb!" Alicia exclaimed throwing her stout arms up in the air.

"Say that girlfriend!" Jackie stated.

"I can't believe that I'm finally getting married." Alicia had always feared that since she was petite and plump that finding a mate would be next to difficult. It seemed that the men she encountered favored skinny women. She learned to allow her inner beauty to shine bright and dynamic personality to lead the way.

"You are lucky. Greg is a great guy," Theresa remarked with a quiet shyness. Her soft gray eyes darted off to avoid direct eye contact with anyone. She felt somewhat anxious. She did not have a college degree or the fancy job title like the rest in the group. She only wanted to fit in and hoped the other ladies were as friendly as Alicia.

"I know. He is wonderful. His proposal was right on time. I've always wanted to be a June bride. I know that sounds corny, but I like tradition and stability. I guess that's why I work as an accountant. Everything has to be exact."

"I hear you girl. I have finally admitted to myself that I'm a perfectionist. But I can do without the numbers." Jackie knew her perfectionism resulted from not wanting anything to be noticeably out of place. She did not like to draw attention to herself, especially any negative unwanted attention.

"Girl you are borderline obsessive-compulsive," Alicia teased Jackie.

"Alicia, what colors have you chosen for the wedding?" Tina chimed in. Tina was bordering on six feet tall and slim like a cover-girl model. She was bold and beautiful. Her dark chocolate complexion was smooth like whipped butter. Her demeanor was always poised and self-assured. Her towering presence commanded attention like a drill sergeant every time she walked into a room.

"I'm thinking about chocolate and champagne."

"Oh, sweetie. I love it! Those colors are trés chic," Stacy stated with her usual perky personality. She was the happy go lucky one of the bunch. She talked to everyone like she always talked to the kids in her first grade class. Stacy owned a classic style, clean cut cropped hair, and simply sweet and petite.

"Isn't chocolate sort of dark for the summertime?" Jackie asked with a hint of cynicism.

"Where are you going on your honeymoon?" Tiffany asked trying to keep the focus on Alicia and away from Jackie's jealous comment. She knew that her friend always liked the attention for herself even if she did not want to admit it. She knew, with Jackie, that it was all about *me...me...me.*

"Well, I think he is planning on St. Thomas. But, he won't say. He wants to surprise me! Isn't that sweet? As long as there is clear blue water and sandy beaches, so I can sport the new bikinis in the day. And of course, the sexy lingerie for the night time." Alicia had visited the gym every day since the engagement. She did not want too much extra skin bouncing in unwanted areas.

"Ok, everyone is done eating their lunch? If so, let's go shopping. I'm ready to move around," Jackie remarked trying not to sound annoyed at all of the attention that Alicia was receiving. She desperately wanted the attention for herself. She could not wait for the day when Kevin dropped to one to knee, recited those magical words, and crowned her with a three-carat princess cut diamond ring. She knew precisely what she wanted and how she wanted it.

CHAPTER 11 - FIREWORKS

The crew canvassed the French Quarters searching for souvenirs and trinkets. The narrow streets were lined with street vendors, tap dancers, jazz musicians, and tourists darting in and out of the tiny shops searching for trinkets. The shelves in the shops displayed a multitude of hot sauces, Mardi Gras beads, feathered masks, and even voodoo chicken feet.

The street was calling; Bourbon Street that is. The girls walked back to their hotel, changed into their party clothes, and strolled down the Street to the House of Blues. The sexy, new artist Brian Cole was scheduled to perform center stage.

"This is so exciting," Jackie stated. "We are going to blow the roof off this place." She donned her black mini halter dress and sassy sling-back shoes. Everything in her suitcase was newly purchased. The shopping mall was a temptation she could not turn away. She made her weekly trips in secret; she did not want the usual scolding from Tiffany about maintaining a budget.

"I can't believe that we are actually in the Big Easy," Stacy commented with the innocence of a ten year old. Her voice high pitched like someone who had just sucked air from a helium balloon.

"I'm happy that all of my girlfriends are here with me to celebrate, even my new friend Theresa!" Alicia exclaimed as she embraced Theresa with a sisterly hug. Theresa smiled a shy smile in response.

The ladies located a table directly in front of the stage. The formed a ring around the table like giddy giggling girl scouts at a campfire. They huddled close to talk to each above the blaring music playing in the background.

"You know we wouldn't miss this weekend for the world!" Tina yelled out.

"I love coming home, especially to New Orleans. There is so much excitement. The people are so friendly," Tiffany added.

"When is Brian Cole coming on? He can sing to me all night. Kevin bought the CD and that is all we listen too. 'All Night Long' is his favorite song," Jackie exclaimed. She bounced up and down in her chair mimicking a dance move.

"My boyfriend's name is Kevin also. What a coincidence," Theresa stated with an air of innocence. She tossed her auburn hair back over her shoulder.

A knot formed in Jackie's stomach at the sound of Kevin's name being spoken through another woman's voice. She pushed the thought out of her mind that it could possibly be the same Kevin. Her Kevin would never associate with the likes of Theresa.

"As a matter of fact, he even likes the same song," Theresa added. "We went dancing last weekend at Club Trophy."

"Oops. Seems like Kevin either has a clone or he is tipping out," Tina stated. "Jackie, were you and Kevin together last weekend?

"No, it can't be the same Kevin," Jackie snapped back with staunch determination. She knew he would never tip out on her. He was the right man at the right time. All of the gifts, dinners, long walks, long talks, long nights of lovemaking. No, Jackie refused to believe that *her* Kevin was cheating.

"Ok, to clear things up, Theresa, please describe your Kevin," Tiffany asked hoping a description would put Jackie's mind at ease.

Everyone sat nervously on the edge of their wooden chairs. It felt like the heat had been turned up past one hundred degrees. Everyone was smoldering with curiosity.

"It's a common name, a popular song. It could just be a coincidence, sweetie," Stacey interrupted trying to appease Jackie like she always did when her students were out of control.

"Of course. You're right Stacey. I'm jumping to conclusions. Getting all bent out of shape. He loves me. I know he wouldn't cheat on me. We spend a lot of time together. He's very caring and attentive. I just know that he is going to pop the question very soon," Jackie kept talking hoping her mind would ease. She thought *how could he become involved with someone like her, Theresa.* Her mind continued to race back and forth in what seemed like an eternity, but only a minute had passed. *His attitude had changed lately*, she thought. She sipped on her cocktail to moisten her mouth and help ease her mind. She looked at the table; she could not make eye contact with anyone in the group. Shame slowly crept up inside of her.

"He has a smooth caramel skin-tone, dark sexy eyes and soft juicy lips. He is an investment banker and his last name is Carlisle. And yes, he is all of that…"

Jackie jumped up from the table before Theresa finished her sentence. Tiffany immediately followed her darting in and out of the crowd crammed in the restaurant.

"Well I guess he is popping something else or shall I say someone else," Tina commented with her usual nonchalant attitude. She popped her fingers in mid-air for emphasis.

"I can't believe this is happening. It was supposed to be a happy, fun-filled weekend; my weekend. Not male drama," Alicia stated filled with disappointment as she sulked back in her chair.

"I'm sorry Alicia. I didn't mean to cause any drama. I didn't know he was dating anyone else, especially one of your friends. We met one night at happy hour. I never thought he was the kind of guy who double-dipped. He seemed sincere and honest."

"That's a salesman for you. Never can be trusted" Tina

chimed in.

"You are just too blunt," Stacey glared at Tina.

"I'm just keeping it real, girl. The fireworks are setting off early and it's not even the 4th yet."

Jackie felt like a dartboard with hundreds of darts pricking and pounding into her heart. The evening meal made its way north up through her body. She ran for the ladies room and reached an empty stall in the nick of time. Jackie felt like the weight of the world was on her shoulders.

"Jackie it's going to be ok. I know you are hurting right now," Tiffany stated trying to calm her distraught friend.

"Tiff, you don't understand…it hurts…I can't believe he lied. I trusted him. I loved him."

"Before you jump to any conclusions, call him. Talk to him and find out if what she is saying is true."

"Whatever…it's true. How else would she know that much personal detail about him?"

"True, but calm down. Don't let his foolishness upset you. Why don't we go back to the hotel and talk it over. You can call Kevin, once we get to the hotel, and talk about it. I'll let Alicia and the others know we are leaving." Tiffany zigzagged back to the table where the crew sat waiting to hear the news. She did not have the guts to look at Theresa, even though she knew it was not her fault. She was trapped in the middle of a muddy mess, like being stranded in the murky waters of the Mississippi.

"Hey ladies, Jackie and I are going back to the hotel." She picked up their purses.

"How is she doing?" Alicia asked with a concerned and confused look on her face.

"She's ok…just very upset. You know how she is. Everything has to be perfect."

"I understand. We'll see you two back at the hotel. Let her have some time to cool down." Alicia stated.

"I didn't mean any harm. I'm sorry to have crashed the party,"

Theresa stated with concern and empathy in her voice. "Kevin never told me had girlfriend. And I just assumed that he was available."

"Obviously, he didn't tell either of you anything," Tina commented.

"I thought he was a nice guy. He was always friendly," Stacey added.

"I guess too friendly it looks like. He wanted to sail his boat around the world and drop anchor at his pleasure," Tina offered.

"Well, Theresa don't worry about it. Everything will work itself out," Alicia stated trying to pacify and calm her friend. "Is Jackie going to call him?"

"Yeah, after we arrive at the hotel, she said she'll call him to find out what the real deal is."

"I need to call him too. And find out what the real the deal is. He has a lot of explaining to do. But should we believe him. I mean if he's been lying to both of us all of this time, what makes us think he will be honest when he is confronted."

"Maybe we should all leave? Stacey questioned the group. "Besides, I'm not in a partying mood anymore."

"I paid for this ticket…and I want to hear and see Brian Cole perform on this stage tonight," Tina commented defiantly. "We all don't need to go the hotel and sulk. I mean, I feel her pain, but I really think she needs some time to cool off and work this mess out."

"Tina, just stay right where you are. Jackie doesn't need your sarcasm or your bad attitude right now. She is going through enough," Tiffany replied with enough force to knock the wind out of Tina.

Jackie had already called a cab to drive her back to the hotel before Tiffany returned. Nothing looked or felt real to Jackie as she slumped down in the backseat of the taxi. Her mind was jarred so far from reality that she barely managed to remember the name of the hotel. As the cab driver sped off through the French Quarters, Jackie realized that what was supposed to be a fun girlfriend weekend getaway, turned out to be a disastrous weekend getaway with Kevin's other girlfriend. Kevin, the man she thought she would marry and have his children; Kevin, the man of her dreams.

She moved as if she was in a vacuum that sucked away her insides. Everything felt tight and constricted. Even the simple task of breathing was labored. She heard voices, but the vacuum sucked the sound into the distance. Jackie realized that, as she replayed the scene over again in her mind, he had lied. *He lied.*

Jackie and Tiffany climbed the staircase to their second floor hotel room. Before the room door could slam shut behind them, Jackie angrily punched the numbers on her cell phone to dial Kevin. She punched each number like a heavyweight boxer jabbing at his opponent, fast and furious.

"Hello," Kevin answered his phone oblivious to the altercation that had just occurred. Unaware that hell's fury had been unleashed and headed in his direction. Kevin sat at the restaurant bar watching his favorite team, the Wolverines in the NBA playoffs.

"I hate you!" Jackie screamed. The words echoed throughout the room bouncing from the ceiling to the floor to each of the four walls searching for their unsuspecting target. The words were sharp and deadly.

"What…what's wrong sweetheart?" Kevin attempted unsuccessfully to calm Jackie.

"What's wrong? How about…Theresa, that's what's wrong." Jackie stood stiffly in the middle of her hotel room. Her arm flagged furiously up and down.

"Theresa who? I don't know what or who you are talking about." Kevin walked outside once he realized that this call was not going to end quickly.

"How about Theresa your other woman?"

"Baby, I don't know any Theresa. I'm telling you the truth." Kevin nervously rubbed his hand over his head.

"Well she knows you and knows you very well according to

her." Jackie had landed her hand on her hip.

"I'm serious. I don't know a Theresa," Kevin's voice began to crack as it dawned on him that maybe, just maybe, Jackie had met his new friend, Theresa. The thought had never entered his mind that the two women's path would ever cross. After all, they lived in one of the largest cities. "Aren't you in New Orleans this weekend with Tiffany and Alicia celebrating her bachelorette party?"

Kevin felt like his world was shrinking and caving in around him. He thought he knew all of Jackie's girlfriends, and they knew him, so her weekend away with the girls was no big deal. She was off the radar for the weekend. He never assumed that when Theresa informed him that she was also unavailable for the weekend that the two women were together. He vaguely remembered Theresa reminding him that she was invited to New Orleans by her supervisor. He never questioned the details of the trip. He assumed it was work related.

"Yes, I am. And also on this trip is Tina, Stacey, and Theresa…your other woman."

"Look Jackie, I told you that I don't know a Theresa. What does she look like…what's her last name. Don't explode on a brotha without the facts." Kevin paced back and forth on the patio of the restaurant.

"Oh, I know the facts. You lied. Plain and simple." Jackie pointed her figure like she was pointing directly at him.

"Can we talk about this when you get back?" Kevin pleaded. His phone was ringing with an incoming call…Theresa.

"Whatever. I'll see you first thing when I'm back at home." Jackie gave once last punch to the phone to end the call.

CHAPTER 12 - PAST MEETS PRESENT

Robert drove up to the circular drive in front of the glass and steel office tower. His metallic silver Mercedes sparkled in the noonday sun. His cell phone was plastered to his ear as he talked and tapped his stubby fingers on the wood grained steering wheel while he waited for Tiffany to exit the building for their usual Thursday lunch date.

Tiffany walked through the glass revolving door and at first sight; Robert instantly tugged at his silk necktie as heat consumed his body. The cold air, blasting from the air conditioner, did not cool him off while watching Tiffany walk towards the car. His infatuation with her beauty had only escalated since he first noticed her. His eyes pierced through the red candy apple colored sweater dress, that clung to her body, as he visualized her wearing only the pink lace bra and panty set he purchased as a gift for her.

A smile instantly came across his face as she opened the car door, eased into the black leather seat, smiled sweetly, and mouthed a simple 'Hello'.

"Hi sweetheart," Robert responded. "You look delicious just like the other night." Their relationship has escalated to include a regular

Tuesday night visit at her apartment lasting up into the late night hours. The routine was written in stone – an intimate evening on Tuesdays and lunch on Thursdays and frequent phone calls in between. The phone calls lasted for hours. No topic was off limits. They shared dreams, hopes, successes, and failures. Robert shared with Tiffany the dreams he had of one day becoming an actor. Ever since his first performance in his high school play, he had the acting fever. But his father would not hear of it. He traded in his desire for Hollywood glitz and glam for the liquid gold of oil and gas.

"You say that all of the time." Tiffany reached in the glove compartment and pulled out her spare pair of sunglasses.

"Well, it's true," Robert commented as he gently stroked her cheek with the back of his hand.

"It's time for a new line," she said smiling.

"I think that one works just fine. After all, you're blushing."

"I'm not," Tiffany playfully responded.

"Your cheeks are as rosy as the color of that sassy dress you're wearing."

"You like my new dress. Jackie and I went shopping. She needed retail therapy after the New Orleans fiasco. I needed some therapy too after that drama story. It was like co-starring in a soap opera." Tiffany started to enjoy shopping with Jackie, especially since Robert gave her cash on a frequent basis.

"You can always call me for therapy…any kind of therapy…you name it. I aim to please," Robert stated with a Cheshire cat grin spread across his plump face.

"Where are we going for lunch? Tiffany asked in an effort to change the subject.

"Why don't we skip lunch and finish what we started the other night?" Robert asked hoping Tiffany would oblige his request.

"No, you'll just have to wait," she stated emphatically. "Besides one hour is not enough time for me to work some more of my magic on you," she added with a hint of sensuality in her voice.

"Well, I guess lunch it is. How about Trevino's? I had a lunch meeting there a week ago. A very nice place. I know you'll like it."

"Ok. You know what I like," Tiffany commented with a mischievous undertone.

Robert drove up to the valet parking station and the two exited the vehicle and proceeded to the maître d' to be seated. He gently placed his hand in the small of Tiffany's back. She sighed softly as the warmth from his hand radiated throughout her body.

Tiffany often expressed her desire for more time, but Robert always had an excuse – a business meeting, a business trip, or just a restful weekend – alone. He always told her it was his alone time or, sometimes, the excuse was time with the guys. She had grown weary standing on second base. The relationship had progressed, but not as she had visualized in her daydreams. Initially, she was hesitant about pursuing an affair with Robert, but the sparks gradually ignited. His charm and witty personality won her over. He did offer some reprieve from the monotony that consumed her life.

The dark mahogany wood structures caste dark shadows throughout the restaurant. Conversations were muted. The corner booth, which served as an intimate shelter for the two, was dimly lit. As they talked and looked over their menus, a dark-blonde gentleman walked up to their table.

"Hi, Robert," the gentleman said.

"Jack, hello. I'm surprised to see you here. Are you in town on business?"

"It's always business. That's my life. I had mediation this morning."

"Jack you need to relax. Take some time off."

"Have fun like you?" Jack stated nodding in Tiffany's direction.

"Jack, allow me to introduce, Tiffany Guillory," Robert said very formal as if Tiffany was his assistant and not his companion. Jack was amazed and stunned with her beauty. She reminded him of a lover from many years ago.

"Hello," Tiffany said with sweet innocence. "It is nice to meet you," she said as she extended her hand to shake Jack's hand while looking at him with her hazel eyes. Jack thought to himself, *those eyes are familiar, and they carry a friendly warmth; such a pretty, innocent face.*

"Robert, do you mind if I join you? I'm not up to dining alone. That's the bad thing about business trips, usually you're alone. I'm glad I ran into you and Tiffany."

Robert attempted to conceal the annoyance that he was feeling. He did not want to lose any precious time he had with Tiffany, especially talking about business.

"Not at all. Please have a seat. I'm sure Tiffany won't mind either."

"Of course not. It is nice to finally meet one of Robert's business associates," Tiffany stated eyeing Robert out the corner of her eye.

Jack gazed at Robert as his male and fatherly instinct flared up. He thought *what a jerk taking advantage of this young lady, playing upon her gullibility.* He never thought Robert's shrewd business techniques spilled over into his personal life, but obviously there were no boundaries. Jack thought *where is this young lady's father?* He should have warned her about men like Robert. He wanted to expose Robert's loathsome behavior, but he decided against interfering in business that had nothing to do with him. Besides, what could he say to subtly warn this sweet young lady?

"Tiffany, you know my father always told me to be careful of the company you keep."

"Jack that was cruel…'Be careful'. What am I? The big bad wolf in the forest? I thought we were friends, business partners at the least," Robert commented attempting to deflect Jack's advice.

"Robert, don't take it personally, unless the shoe fits. I just thought it's a good piece of advice to share with Tiffany. Wouldn't you agree?" Robert smiled faintly at Jack as the two men exchanged spiteful glances.

Tiffany sat looking back and forth between the two men. Her intuition kicked in and wandered what was Robert hiding from her. Not sure how to respond to Jack's comment, she simply answered,

"Yes sir. I'll remember that."

"Have we met before Tiffany?" Jack asked to change the subject.

"No, sir. I don't think so. I'm sure I would have remembered."

"You are a charming young lady and very pretty too. You remind me of my daughters. It is uncanny the resemblance – your smile reminds me of my youngest Julie, and your eyes are bold and beautiful like my oldest daughter, Erica."

"Thank you Mr. Jack. My looks are inherited from my mother. I never knew my father, so I can't honestly say what looks are from his genes," Tiffany responded with modesty.

"I'm sure your mother is a lovely lady," Jack stated.

"Yes, she is."

Jack could not shake the eerie feeling that he knew this young lady. Her lovely, delicate features grabbed a hold of him and would not let go. The thoughts tugged at him like a ribbon being untied from around a beautiful gift. The similarities to his daughters were striking and uncanny. Her sweet, charming smile also resembled someone else.

"Tiffany, where does such a pretty young lady like you call home?" Jack asked with his gentle Southern accent, reminiscent of the days of walking down a boulevard lined with Magnolia trees.

"I'm from Sunset Bayou in Louisiana."

Jack nearly choked on the iced tea he had just swallowed. *Sunset Bayou* he thought, it couldn't be. Not in a million years. Jack's mind raced back in time to that steamy night when him and Luella were enraptured with infatuation and clung to each other as they rocked each other like a boat tossing back and forth on the stormy sea.

"Are you ok?" Robert asked.

"Yes, I'm fine." Jack regained his composure and continued, "I was just thinking it's a small world. You know Robert, I'm from Louisiana. But you probably don't know that Sunset Bayou is just a few miles up the road from my hometown. Maybe that is why Tiffany looks so familiar. Her features are reminiscent of a Louisiana lady I knew in my younger days."

"What city is your hometown?" Tiffany asked.

"Lafayette."

"Oh, wow. It is a small world. My mama and I would go to Lafayette all the time to shop, since there isn't anything to do in Sunset Bayou. Mama also worked in Lafayette at Petre's Café for a long time before Mr. Petre passed away. She loved working at the café. She's always talking about the good old days. Did you ever eat at Petre's?"

"Maybe once or twice."

"No one can eat just once or twice at Petre's. My favorite was the dirty rice and peach cobbler."

Now, Jack tugged at his necktie and cleared his throat as his cheeks turned a fiery red. The conversation was taking off on a course he had not expected. The past was now very much in the present sitting right next to him. For the first time, he was at a loss for words. That was unusual for the savvy, sharp-tongued lawyer such as himself. All words had escaped him. He never thought, in a million years, he would come face to face with this young lady.

"You're right; the food was delicious at Petre's. One of my favorites was the dirty rice also."

"My mama can make a delicious dirty rice. In fact it was her recipe that Petre used," Tiffany responded with pride.

"Really. What's your mother's name?"

"Luella Guillory. She worked as a waitress at the café."

Jack coughed and cleared his throat when he heard Luella's name. He thought *surely it could not be the same person*. He regained his composure, again, and quickly stated, "Well, I must be leaving now. It was a pleasure meeting and talking with you, Tiffany. Robert, I'll be in touch about the Tetco deal."

"Sure Jack. It was great seeing you. Take care," Robert said cordially. Excited that Jack was leaving, he could now enjoy the remainder of his time with Tiffany.

"Oh no, look at the time. I have to get back to work. I can't wait to call Mama and tell her about Mr. Jack. What is his last?"

"Fontenot. Jack Fontenot," Robert answered. He glanced at his watch and with great disappointment, signaled for the waiter to bring the check. "I guess it is time to go. I'll call you later."

Tiffany wrapped her wet hair in a fluffy towel to soak up the excess water. The smell of the jasmine shampoo filled the air of her tiny one bedroom apartment. Friday night's usual routine was underway. Light the spiced-pear candle, pour a glass of white wine, order Chinese takeout, turn on the radio to listen to the R&B hits, and finally relax.

Since Jackie started dating Kevin, their girl's night out on Friday's was canceled. And she did not even bother phoning Robert because her calls went straight into voicemail. She finally decided it was time for a long talk. She wanted more – more time, more affection, more of him.

The comment that Jack made continued to linger in her mind, *Be careful of the company keep*. Robert appeared to be a nice man; even though, he was evasive at times. She hoped she had not become entangled in a triangle like Jackie.

The spa-like atmosphere created the quiet time Tiffany craved for. The hustle and flow of the city was taking its toll on her. Often she wanted to pack up and head back to the simple life of Sunset.

Meeting Jack the other day intensified that feeling. His Southern accent and charm stirred up deep emotions. Tiffany dialed the familiar number that had been existence since before she was born.

"Hi Mama!"

"Hi baby," Luella responded excitedly.

"What are you doing?"

"Not much sweetie pie. Enjoying a relaxing evening and watching these crazy television shows. What are you doing calling me on a Friday night? I thought you were dating somebody." Luella padded her way to the living room and plopped down on the couch.

"Yes, I am. But he had something else to do."

"Something else to do. Honey you should always be priority number one."

"Mama, it's not that serious," she responded hoping to downplay the relationship and avoid the inevitable line of questioning that always occurred.

"How long have you known him?" Luella began drilling Tiffany like she was a police sergeant. She wanted details – name, occupation, height, weight, eye color, and hair color – all the necessary elements to sketch an image of the mystery man dating her daughter.

"A few months," Tiffany responded with a short answer; even though, she knew the answer would not satisfy Luella's curiosity.

"What are a few months? I want a number."

"About six months," Tiffany answered while bracing herself for the inevitable question she knew would be asked. Luella was very predictable, after all, she had lived an uninterrupted existence in the same house, same city, and same job for many years until forced to seek another one.

"Six months. Tiff, that is long enough to be serious. When am I going to meet this fellow?"

"I don't know, maybe when you finally come to visit me. You know Sunset is not going to fall apart or disappear if you leave for a couple of days. That reminds me; I met a nice gentleman yesterday. He is a friend of Robert's who is from Lafayette. He said that he had eaten at Petre's, you might know him. His name is Jack Fontenot. Do you know him?" Tiffany cleverly changed the subject from the present to the past.

At that instant, time froze, and Luella could not respond even if she had the answer to a million dollar question. Never, in her lifetime, did she think she would hear that name spoken by her baby girl - *Jack Fontenot.*

"Uh…maybe that was a long time ago. What does he look like?" She finally answered after what seemed like eternity. Luella did not need a description. The soft blue eyes, the inviting smile, his charming Southern accent, the gentle touch of his hands. Luella did not hear another word spoken by Tiffany. She sat listening absently. She heard Tiffany's voice, but the words spoken after the initial shock eluded her.

"Mama…Mama are you listening to me?"

"Yeah, baby, I'm listening." Luella thought *I really don't need to listen. I know too well what he looks like. What he feels like. I see him every time I look at you.*

CHAPTER 13 - THE MIND IS A BATTLEFIELD

Dark scaly hands reached out to grab Jackie. She dodged them as she shifted to the right. She screamed, at least she thought she screamed. She felt her lips move but heard no audible sound escape from her encircle-shaped mouth. More hands moved in front of her. She waved, shoved, and flapped her hands to push away the dry, flaky hands with the rounded nail-bitten fingertips that moved towards her. Jackie jumped, sitting straight up in the middle of the cherry wood queen-sized sleigh bed, and realized it was all a bad dream.

The sheets were tangled and jumbled, half draped across the bed and half fallen on the floor. Jackie shifted her stiff body so that her shaky legs hung over the side of the bed. She wiped away the cold sweat, which had beaded upon her forehead, and wrapped her arms tightly around her body. She slid her perfectly pedicured feet into her warm, cozy, spa-like, sand-colored slippers. She needed to feel something familiar, something safe, and something stable to ease the tension and calm her nerves. Her mind raced back and forth pondering the significance of the nightmares that disturbed her peaceful nights. Now, another dream had jolted her from a restful sleep and forced her to lay awake and shaken for the remainder of the night.

She staggered toward the oversized picture window in her bedroom and gazed out into the darkness. Jackie leaned her body heavily against the supporting beam that protruded from the wall. The late night had an overcast of clouds sprinkled throughout the sky. The full moon shined brightly behind the veil of condensed vapor suspended in the air. Her mind drifted aimlessly along like the clouds, even though, her desire was to drift back into a peaceful sleep. She turned to gaze at the clock resting on the glass top of her nightstand. Her eyes focused and noticed 4:38 a.m., only four hours before her alarm sounded off with the latest gospel music playing on Gospel 100.7, her other favorite radio station.

She padded across the hardwood floors, to the comfort of her bed, and crawled in between the soft cotton sheets. She wanted nothing more than to free her mind from the dingy, dirty man, who haunted her dreams, before it was time to face the morning sunlight. She balled her body up in a fetus-style, like an unborn baby safely wrapped in their mother's womb.

Before the alarm clock blasted off, the familiar ring tone sounded off at 7:00 a.m. sharp. She glanced at the caller id. It was Kevin.

"Good morning, sleepyhead!" Kevin stated with exuberance.

"Hey, what's up?" Jackie yawned slightly.

"How about you and me head out this morning for breakfast?" Kevin thought to himself *there she goes again with those short answers, but it is early.*

"You know it is Sunday…and Tiff and I are going to church. Why don't you join us? Your soul needs to be saved," Jackie responded with sharp sarcasm.

"I will be glad to join you at church services. Better yet, I'll drive over to pick you up and we can go to lunch after services," Kevin further indulged, desperately trying to move back into Jackie's good graces.

"Sure, you can join us at Sister Soul's. It is our regular after church hangout."

"You drive a hard bargain. Can't a brotha get some alone time?"

"Umm. I'll think about it. In the meantime, I'll see you at 10:30 a.m., sharp. Not a minute late," Jackie concluded sternly.

Since the New Orleans fiasco, Jackie did not what to think about neither Kevin nor their relationship. Everything was up in the air, their past – was it real, their present – was it worth it, and their future – was definitely on shaky ground. She searched and prayed for the will to forgive Kevin, but her trust in him was eroded. The nightmares and the Kevin drama, Jackie knew she had to collect enough courage to face the facts and look truth in the face.

Not wanting to be late herself, she turned on the water in the shower. The steam from the hot water relaxed her tense muscles, but not the stressful thoughts that resided in her mind. Memories and flashbacks flooded her mind like a rushing river released with a fury. Jackie felt like she was a sinking ship; sinking into the depths of darkness. The weight of the revelation of the incident, which happened many nights long ago in the midnight hours, weighed her down like an anchor.

She braced herself against the damp tile of the shower. The hot water continued to stream down and soothe her tired body. Her world was unraveling – the nightmares about her daddy, the fiasco with Kevin, the deadlines at work, and the pressures of perfection.

Jackie padded to her closet while wrapped in her bathrobe. Her closet was the epitome of a fashion boutique. Clothes arranged by color, season, day, and evening. She reached for her navy silk crepe full-flowing dress. Jackie pulled her long ebony-colored hair into a ponytail, dusted on her makeup, and adorned her neck with Meme's pearls.

Just as she glanced at herself in the mirror, for one final look, the doorbell rang. She thought to herself, *I can't believe he is on time for a change.*

"Good morning sweetheart," Kevin pronounced like making a grand proclamation.

"Good morning," Jackie responded in kind, but without the matching enthusiasm.

"I thought you might like some breakfast, so I brought bagels and coffee." Kevin marched in and pecked Jackie on the cheek.

"Thank you, so much. That was very thoughtful of you," Jackie knew he was still trying to regain her favor after the New Orleans catastrophe and she planned to squeeze every ounce of repentance out of him.

"We have time to eat and have a cup of coffee before we leave," Kevin stated as he made his way to the kitchen to pop the bagels in the toaster oven. He put the two cups of coffee on the breakfast bar.

"Well, ok. I am hungry…and I don't want my stomach growling in church." She trailed behind him to the kitchen.

"Did I tell you how pretty you look?" Kevin asked with a gleaming smile.

"No, you didn't." She blushed and batted her eyelashes.

"Well, you do. Are those the pearls that belonged to your grandmother?"

"Yes, they are. They were a wedding gift to her from her mother. I love collectibles that have a special history to them."

"Just like the quilt on your bedroom wall."

"Yeah, like the quilt. Hey you are looking handsome yourself," Jackie stated to change the conversation. She did not want to discuss the past or the people from the past at that moment.

Kevin modeled his dark gray pin stripe suit while he tugged on his deep purple necktie. "Here is your blueberry bagel. You can spread your own cream cheese. I know that you like only a certain amount."

"Are you making fun of me? I like what I like and that's that."

"You know, it is ok to be flexible…to let go and let loose sometimes." Kevin slid across the kitchen floor attempting to perform a mock New Edition dance move.

"I try. I'm just a very traditional person," Jackie replied. She topped of her bagel with a dollop of cream cheese.

"You are a perfectionist. That's what you are. Everything and everybody in life is not perfect. I know that I'm not."

Jackie knew the direction that the conversation was heading, and it was his way of making excuses for his infidelity. "Kevin, I do not hold everyone up to a high standard." She sipped on her coffee.

"Bull, that is a load of cramp and you know it." He tapped his hand on the counter top.

"Look I don't want to discuss this with you this Sunday morning. Let's finish our bagels and coffee so we can leave. I don't want to keep Tiff waiting." Jackie bit off a large piece of bagel as another attempt to avoid the conversation.

"You know we have to talk about what happened in New Orleans sometime," Kevin commented staring point blank at Jackie. He was persistent. She swallowed hard and took another sip of her coffee. The java helped to warm her insides and calm her nerves.

"Fine. Let's talk. What is your explanation?" Jackie eyed Kevin waiting for his response.

"Well, I met Theresa one night at happy hour. It was during one of those times when you kept pushing a brotha away." The two remained in the kitchen standing with the breakfast between them.

"Oh, so it's my fault? I never meant to push you away." Jackie pointed at her chest.

"No, it's not your fault. I'm sorry, if I didn't understand. One minute you're all into me and the next minute you're not. I could've easily thought that you were dating someone else."

"You know I love you and would never cheat on you, but obviously you don't feel the same way," Jackie firmly stated with tears building in her eyes.

"I do love you, Jackie. But every time we made love, afterwards, you would become distant like you were having second thoughts or just not interested. What's up?" Kevin held his arms in midair.

"I didn't realize that I was coming across as distant. Why didn't you ask me about it, instead of looking for love with someone else?" Jackie mustered as much strength as she could to keep the tears in her eyes.

"I don't love Theresa or anyone else. And I told her that we couldn't be friends anymore. I love you, Jackie. I know you're thinking how can you say that?" Kevin looked directly into Jackie's eyes. He wanted her to know that he was serious.

"Right, how can you say I love you, after what happened..." Jackie braced herself on the counter for support.

"But, let me finish. I expect my lady to be all into me and show devotion, admiration, and some understanding," Kevin continued.

"I've always tried to support you. I thought I was expressing my love for you," Jackie pleaded.

"Well, I guess our lines of communication are crossed and we need to work it out."

"Yes, we do," Jackie concluded as she grabbed her purse and Bible to walk out of the door. Kevin sighed and followed behind her.

New Tabernacle Missionary Baptist greeted members and visitors each Sunday morning; with dusty red bricks, rows of pink, purple and yellow petunias, illuminated stained-glass windows, and of course, smiling faces of the congregation. Jackie and Kevin walked in silence to the glass doors. The first smiling face that greeted them was Sister Armstrong dressed in her form-fitting scarlet-colored suit with the fur trim collar. Jackie forced herself to hold back the laughter that brewed in her when she recalled the story Tiffany told her about the gambling chips.

"Good morning!" Sister Armstrong exclaimed with a bright, cheery smile plastered across her face.

"Good morning, Sister Armstrong. How are you doing?" Jackie replied with a straight face.

"Oh, I'm blessed and highly favored," Sister Armstrong responded with an air of righteous indignation and her Bible clutched closely to her chest.

"Yes, ma'am. I'm sure you are as well as everybody else, since we are all God's children." Jackie allowed a faint smile to escape from her lips.

"Right you are young lady. But you know some of us are more than others; those of us who walk in the ways of the good book. I always walk in the ways of the Lord; on the straight and narrow. The ways of the Lord shall never depart from me and his words shall continually be upon my lips," Sister Armstrong elaborated.

"You have a blessed day, Sister Armstrong. We're going to find a seat," Jackie replied with a fake smile tugging on Kevin's arm.

Once the couple was out of earshot of Sister Armstrong, Jackie laughed and Kevin looked at her like a mad woman gone insane.

"What is so funny?" Kevin asked.

"She is funny. Tiffany told me about an incident when the two of them were in the ladies room, and Sister Armstrong's purse fell, and casino chips rolled onto the floor. She was scurrying around like a little rat trying to hide her evidence," Jackie explained to Kevin as she tried to contain herself from laughing uncontrollably.

"Women. Ya'll are not right. Give the old lady a break. Maybe she's had a hard life."

"She shouldn't walk around proclaiming that she is holier than thou, like she's better than everybody else...being hypocritical. I understand we all have our past secrets and skeletons, but come on...she can tone it down a bit."

"Ok. I agree on that, but she is old...and probably all she knows is the Lord. And she knows how to work the slot machine," Kevin replied with a smirk on his face.

"Why are you defending her anyway? You don't even know her," Jackie irritatingly stated as she led the way to her and Tiffany's usual pew.

"Because I know that people make mistakes...like me...like you also. We can't stand in judgment of others. I know you are thinking that well 'she is judging us' but like I said she is old and probably set in her ways. So give her a break."

"Are you trying to get to the point where you are asking me to give you a break?" Jackie whispered.

"Well…yes, since you brought it up." Kevin wanted to take advantage of every opportunity. He knew in church there would be no loud discusses or heated debates. The odds were in his favor.

"We'll have to finish this discussion later. Here comes Tiff, scoot over."

Tiffany joined the duo just as they stood to sing their opening worship hymn. She glanced at Jackie sideways with the expression as to why Kevin was with her. Jackie ignored her friend's questioning look and tried to focus on the choir. She did not have the energy, or the desire, for any heated, or in depth, conversations.

The choir finished their selection leading into Pastor Dalton's sermon. He approached the honey oak podium embellished with a golden cross spread across the front. He opened his Bible and read aloud the scripture for the morning's sermon.

"Saints please open your Bibles to 1 Thessalonians, chapter 5, verses 16 and 17. Follow along with me as I gladly recite the words of our dear Lord, 'Be joyful always; pray continually; give thanks in all circumstances, for this is God's will for you in Christ Jesus.'

"The sermon this morning focuses upon how our mind can be a battlefield. The scripture tells us to be thankful in all circumstances, but I know that most of you are wandering how you can be thankful when worry, doubt, depression, and anxiety are all attacking your mind. Circumstances and situations arise in our lives day in and day out, forcing us to stray off course and not keep our focus on the Lord…to rejoice in his glory and receive his mercy. The mind with all of its impulses and signals and stimuli of the world wants to distract us from our spiritual focus. Our focus is to be thankful about what the Lord has provided in our lives. Whether good or bad, our purpose is to praise the Lord and be thankful in any situation."

Pastor Dalton sighed and continued with, "I see intense pain and hurt on some of your faces; hurt that you have been holding onto for years, hurt that you use as a crutch to carry you each day, hurt that no longer needs to control your life. Do I have a witness?" Shouts of amen's and hallelujah's reverberated throughout the sanctuary.

Jackie shifted uneasily as she heard the preacher's words. She was guilty of carrying around years of hurt; carrying the burden around that was hidden just beneath the surface. Jackie could never bring herself to tell the truth to any of the women who she loved when they lived upon the green and glorious earth. She did not want to see eyes of blame, hear words of disbelief, so she buried the ugly truth six feet in her soul, and in her mind. She covered it up with a hardened heart, hallowed eyes, painstaking perfectionism, and a pretentious smile.

Pastor Dalton continued with his fiery sermon. "Even though mankind has experienced hurt since the fall of man in the garden of Eve, we know that we have a Savior who has redeemed us; a Savior who has paid the price for the sins of the world, so that we don't have to carry the burdens around day after day. We can rejoice and be thankful. We can reach up and God's hand is there, full of power and glory, illuminating a light of hope and peace. Let me encourage you as children of the almighty to let go of the weapons of the world. Release yourself from worry, doubt, anxiety, depression, and arm yourself with peace, happiness, joy, and love."

Even though, Eve had eaten of the forbidden fruit from the tree of wisdom, Jackie did not need to eat any fruit to know the difference between right and wrong. She knew at the core of her soul, at the center of her heart, and at the center of her mind that what her daddy did to her was wrong; the wrong touch in the wrong spot. Jackie had no one to tell the horrible truth that surfaced to the forefront of her mind after being buried underneath piles of rubble.

Even after the car crash that led to the death of her mother and father, she could not bear to think about the unimaginable deeds. She could not stand to speak the dreadful truth. Besides, there was still no one to tell. She could not break Grandma Meme's heart with the filthy reality that her only son had committed the perverted sin of indecent exposure, inappropriate touching, and use of offensive language. No, she carried the weight of the burden inside her, which weighed her down like an anchor that docked a ship at port.

She thought about confiding in Tiffany, but could not bear the pain of reciting the awful truth. No, Jackie was determined to take the truth to her grave. But fate would not have it. Like the tide washing in the debris buried at sea, the truth washed up to the surface and overtook Jackie with all its force and fury.

Jackie could no longer force back the tears. The sobs poured out uncontrollably while she rocked back and forth mimicking the rocking motion of Meme that night on the porch after the car crash. She released the pain, the hurt that had controlled her life for many years. She did not worry about perfection at the present moment. She did not worry about the folks in the congregation. Tiffany and Kevin were both taken by surprise. Neither one of them had ever seen Jackie lose control.

"What's wrong with the poor child?" Sister Armstrong asked as she walked by with a nosy curiosity written all over her face.

"She's fine," Tiffany replied with fake smile. "We have everything under control."

"Umm hmm. I'm sure you do. Why don't we walk her out to the ladies' room so she can better compose herself?" Sister Armstrong suggested.

"Yes ma'am," Tiffany hesitantly replied to Sister Armstrong's command as she lifted Jackie by the arm from her seat. She did not particularly want to be in the company of Sister Armstrong, especially since she was not certain of the circumstances that had her friend frazzled and upset.

As the ladies exited the sanctuary, Sister Armstrong gave a quick, sharp glance at Kevin. She murmured in a low tone, "I hope she is not pregnant."

Kevin was stunned. He did not know what to say or how to react to this woman. Just earlier he had defended her against the judgments of Jackie, but now he saw the truth.

Tiffany overheard Sister Armstrong's blatant comment and forced herself to hold back the truth about the casino chips that was on the edge of her tongue. After the ladies entered the lounge area, Tiffany contemplated her words carefully before confronting Sister Armstrong.

"How can you stand there in judgment of everyone when you have your own skeletons?"

Tiffany eyed Sister Armstrong as she vehemently questioned the elderly lady. She helped Jackie to sit on the golden suede sofa. Tiffany reached for the box of Kleenex off the countertop and handed a coupled of tissues to Jackie so she could dry her eyes. Jackie ignored the two women, not having the energy to intervene. She knew when Tiffany wanted to express her thoughts that there was no holding her back. Tiffany was quiet, but a forceful storm buried within her would erupt without a moment's notice if she witnessed any injustice.

"Why that is no way to talk to your elders. I hope your mama taught you better." Sister Armstrong stood up straight with her head held high and her back arched.

"Yes, she did teach me better…better to tell the truth. Have *you* forgotten about *your* casino chips that rolled across the bathroom floor?" Tiffany questioned as she glared defiantly at Sister Armstrong.

Sister Armstrong gave a strong, defiant look back at Tiffany as if to say with her eyes what her mouth did not, 'Mind your business young lady.'

Tiffany ignored Sister Armstrong from that point onward as she turned her attention to her troubled friend. "Jackie, are you ok? What's wrong? Is it Kevin?"

"I need to leave. Can you please ask Kevin to come on and let's go? I need to go home and lie down," Jackie responded just above a whisper. Her breathing was labored like a runner who just finished running a marathon.

Jackie and Kevin sped along the highway towards downtown to Jackie's loft. Silence permeated throughout the car. Neither one said a word. No one knew what to say or how to say it. Jackie was still unsure how to explain to Kevin what was troubling her. He did not know how to ask her again if she was still upset about the ordeal that occurred in New Orleans.

Finally, he asked Jackie, "Do you want to go away for a long weekend? Maybe we need some time away…a change of scenery…have some fun? What do you think?" Kevin asked gripping the steering wheel hoping Jackie would be agreeable.

"Ok, sounds like fun," Jackie responded half-heartedly staring out the window with a blank expression plastered on her face.

"How about a ski trip? Have you ever been skiing before?" Kevin looked back and forth at Jackie and the highway.

"No…sounds like fun." Her words were faint and quick. She leaned her head against the black leather seat.

"It'll be lots of fun…you, me, the snow. We can snuggle in front of the fireplace or keep each other warm with our body heat." Kevin added with a large smile spread across his face.

Jackie perked up and smiled in response to Kevin's comments. "I like the part about the fireplace." Jackie responded. She slowly began the process of burying the truth – again.

"Great…I'll pick out a couple of different spots for us to choose from when you are feeling better. Uh, Jackie is there anything that I should know?" Kevin asked cautiously. The words of Sister Armstrong echoed in the back of his mind, 'I hope she is not pregnant.'

"Not anything you need to concern yourself about."

"If it is about you, then it concerns me. I love you and care about you. Don't keep shutting me out. We just talked about not communicating this morning. I want to help. Talk to me babe."

Jackie wanted to open up to him and confide in him about the horrible nightmares and the ugly truth. But at the moment, she did not have the energy. She wanted to rest. After carrying around the heavy load, she needed rest.

CHAPTER 14 - SPIDER'S WEB

Tiffany gathered her portfolio and left for her 10:00 a.m. meeting with Sandra Cole, the Promise Keepers representative, for the upcoming luncheon to finalize the details. The meeting was expected to last no longer than an hour. After months of meticulous planning, phone calls, emails, face to face meetings, the loose ends were finally being tied. Today's meeting would outline the final details for the program on the day of the luncheon. She also wanted to meet with the mistress of ceremony. The script for the program had to be reviewed and rehearsed.

Tiffany suggested, to the charity representative, that they meet at the hotel where the event was to be held to review the final layout and also for her convenience to meet Robert for their regularly scheduled lunch date. Today she planned to push the issue for more time together. Mama was right. Six months was long enough and long overdue for more quality time. She deserved to be number one. No more excuses or today would be the last date.

"Hello Sandra," Tiffany stated while shaking hands with the Promise Keepers representative. She enjoyed working with Sandra, who was always prompt, detailed and direct. Tiffany marveled at the fact that Sandra was all about business. Every encounter proved to be beneficial. Sandra helped Tiffany escalate the luncheon to a high-scale level she could not have even dreamed.

"Hello Tiffany. It's nice to see you again. I'm excited that we are almost complete with the planning, especially since the event is only a week away!"

"I know. Everyone will be excited at the conclusion of the luncheon. And may I add a very successful luncheon." The ladies chatted while waiting in the main lobby of the hotel for the mistress of ceremonies to join them.

"You've done a wonderful job planning this very special event. I can't wait to tell Mary Beth that she made an excellent choice in choosing you to plan this event," Sandra elaborated.

"Thank you. It has been a pleasure working with you. I'm happy that Mary Beth chose me to plan this event."

"Yes, all the details have been handled exceptionally well; from the invitations to the menu. Oh, here comes Elyse, the mistress of ceremony."

"Great. I can't wait to meet her. I have the script for the program for her."

"Hello, Elyse Carrington. I want to introduce you to Tiffany Guillory, our event planner."

"Hello Mrs. Carrington. It is a pleasure meeting you," Tiffany stated. She could not help but to admire her beauty and graceful posture. There were certain similarities; the smooth butter complexion, the pale blonde hair cascading down her shoulders, the sparkly hazel eyes. It was almost like looking in a mirror or at a long lost sister.

"Please call me Elyse. It is finally nice to meet you Tiffany. Sandra has had nothing but good things to say about you and your work. I know the luncheon is going to be spectacular." The group gravitated to the ballroom to discuss the final details.

"Yes, we are all excited. I have the script here to review with you." Tiffany was anxious to move past the pleasantries and to start business. Time was ticking and she was ready to move on to other things. Her lunch date with Robert and the impending conversation that she intended to have with him.

The ladies wrapped up their review of the final plans and made small talk as they left the hotel ballroom. Tiffany waved good-bye to the two ladies and walked to the hotel restaurant. Robert was already waiting at a table in the corner by the window. The maître d' escorted Tiffany to the table.

"Hello sexy," Robert mouthed with a slick grin.

"Hello to you to," Tiffany replied.

"How was the meeting? Have the other ladies left?"

"Yes, the two other ladies have left. And the meeting went very well. All of the details have been finalized."

"Great. I know that you did an excellent job because you are good at everything you do; and I mean everything," Robert stated while stroking Tiffany's hand.

"You are perverted," Tiffany remarked sarcastically.

Robert leaned over to whisper into Tiffany's ear, "Since we are already in a hotel, how about checking into a room for the remainder of the day. You can tell your boss that your meeting ran longer than expected." He was so enthralled with enticing Tiffany to agree with his plan that he did not notice the lady standing in front of his table.

"Hello Robert," Elyse stated.

Robert almost swallowed his tongue when he looked up and saw his wife standing in front of him.

"Interesting to see you here... and with Tiffany, is it?" Elyse looked at Tiffany with contempt.

Tiffany did not know what to say or what to do. The last name popped in her mind, *Carrington*. She looked at Mrs. Carrington's left hand and the four carat diamond nearly blinded her. All the pieces were falling into place – the limited time together, the unanswered phone calls, the secluded lunch dates, the warning from Mr. Fontenot.

"Yes, Tiffany! Mrs. Carrington...I thought you and Sandra left?"

Tiffany asked frozen with fright.

"Well obviously not. I see you didn't leave either, since you're having a rendezvous with my husband," Elyse stated with fire burning in her eyes.

"Sweetheart, I can explain. Tiffany is helping me to plan an office event. Trust me it is not what it looks like." Robert stood up. He reached for his wife's shoulder in a vain attempt to console her. She jerked her shoulder back out of his reach.

"Don't touch me. And that's not what it looks like. Do you always hold hands during business meetings? Really Robert, give me a break." Her words were sharp and distinct.

"Darling, we were just leaving. Why don't we talk about this later, at home?" He reached one more time for her arm. The cutting look in her eyes spoke the words, *do not touch me.*

"Later...at MY home. Yes we can talk because after this, it will no longer be your home."

"Come on Elyse. Let's go and not make a scene." Sandra walked over to control her friend. Sandra eyed Tiffany scornfully.

Tiffany grabbed her purse and portfolio and rushed out of the restaurant before Robert even had a chance to part his lips. She knew a phone call had already been made to Mary Beth before she even walked out the hotel's door. She had to decide whether she should go back to the office and face the line of fire, or to go home and hide out. She decided to drive back to the office and face the fire sooner than later. After all, she knew that her boss would chew her up and spit her out like she had just eaten a rotten apple.

Tiffany pushed the speed dial button on her cell phone to call Jackie while she sped along the interstate to her office to receive the dreaded pink slip. The ordeal was too much to deal with alone.

"Jackie! Hell has broken loose again!"

"What are you talking about?"

"The man is married," Tiffany yelled.

"Robert...MARRIED...No way. You had no idea. I thought you had all that checked out."

"I thought so too. I want to scream. You know, I just need to move back home where it is calm and quiet. I feel like I've walked into a spider's web," Tiffany lamented. She felt like a tiny boat crashing on the sandy shore and scattering into a million pieces.

"Come on Tiff, you're being irrational. You're upset and not thinking clearly. You don't want to move back to Sunset. I need you to calm down. You are the strong and sensible one," Jackie tried to console her best friend. "Do you always have to be so poetic and dramatic? It's ok, so you got 'tangled in the' what did you say...'life's threads?'" Jackie asked. "Where are you now?"

"I'm on my way back to office...where I know for sure that I'm going to be fired."

"Why are you going to be fired? For dating a married man? I don't get it."

"The man is married to my client who is a friend of my boss? I had a meeting with Sandra and the mistress of ceremonies, who turned out to be Robert's wife. Robert and I met for lunch at the hotel after my business meeting. Sandra and his wife see us snuggled up in a booth at the restaurant. So, you know what happens next...drama!"

"Oooh! Are you sure you want to go back today? Why not wait until tomorrow to let things cool down?"

"No, I want to deal with it now and move on. I'm driving into the parking garage now. I'll let you know what happens."

Tiffany arrived at her desk and sat down to compose herself. She focused on concocting a believable story so that everyone, mainly herself, would survive this fiasco unharmed. The minute after she took a deep breath, Mary Beth was standing in her door. The fumes flamed around her. Her usually rosy-colored cheeks were bright red and her lips were pressed hard.

"I need to see you in my office in ten minutes," Mary Beth demanded and walked off before Tiffany had a chance to part her lips to utter a word.

Tiffany inhaled another deep breath. She looked around her tiny cubicle and knew this was the last time that she would ever be in this little space again. She composed herself and strolled down the hall to Mary Beth's office.

"Come in and have a seat," Mary Beth ordered. "I received a call from Sandra, a few minutes ago, explaining about what happened earlier today. I must say that I am very appalled and very disappointed. I trusted you with one of the biggest accounts that we have, and also an account with a very dear and longtime friend of mine. And to hear of such accusations was very disturbing. I'm in an extremely awkward position Tiffany. You have done such great work during your tenure here, but in light of the circumstances, I have no choice but to terminate you effective immediately."

"Yes ma'am. I understand completely. If I may explain, I had no idea that he was married. There was no evidence that he was married."

"Even if that is the case, and I hope it is, I still have no other choice but to let you go."

"Yes ma'am," Tiffany responded with a heavy heart.

She walked back to her cubicle, and a box was waiting on her desk for her to pack her belongings. The human resources assistant waited outside the entrance to escort her from the building and collect her security badge. Tiffany did not have the heart or the energy to look at the assistant. She could not bear to see another disapproving face stare at her with disgust. She wandered how she was going to move forward from this fiasco. She only wanted to receive love, and look what love gave her – a broken heart, a shattered reputation, and a place in the unemployment line.

CHAPTER 15 - DOUBLE PORTION FOR YOUR SHAME

The morning sun peaked through the stained-glass windows, of New Tabernacle, creating a heavenly glow throughout the sanctuary. The parishioners sat once again for their weekly revival waiting to experience the fullness of God's glory.

Pastor Dalton held up a mirror towards the congregation and asked the members, "What do you see? Before you can look at your brother's or your sister's faults, take a look in this or any mirror. The mirror will reflect the truth. The mirror will reflect plainly and you can rest assured that it will not lie to you." Pastor Dalton paused and took a look around the congregation.

"You will see the plank in your eye, plain as the daylight, before you see the tiny speckle revealed in your brother's eye. Now, I know we have all heard this topic preached before, but we always need a reminder. Some of us need reminding more than others." The congregation sighed in agreement with the Pastor's comments.

"Remember the mirror my dear friends. Some of you might want to carry one with you every day. Some of you already do, but fail to use it; or at least fail to look at your reflection in the light of truth. Remember the mirror; remember your reflection of truth."

Pastor Dalton exhaled a long sigh, and then led into, "Some of us walk around carrying a mirror with a distorted reflection like the house of mirrors at the carnival. Your perception is distorted, disfigured, discolored; a reflection that does not reflect the complete you, the real you, the hidden hurts inside of you. Remember the mirror, your mirror, when you are tempted to judge with your earthly eyes blinded by the prejudices of the world. Your Heavenly Father sees beyond the scope of our limited vision. His vision goes to the depths of the soul, and the corners of the heart. His vision knows no boundaries." He then paused for a moment in order to wipe his forehead which was beginning to drench with sweat.

"If your mirror reflects imperfections, and I'm sure it does, remember my friends, the Lord will restore you double for your shame and double for your pain. God promises us, in his word, written by the prophet Isaiah, 'instead of shame my people will receive a double portion, and instead of disgrace they will rejoice in their inheritance…' Turn with me to Isaiah, chapter 61, verse 7, as we read and reflect on that passage. Regardless of what your mirror reflects, God promises to restore you and bring you closer to him. He loves you unconditionally," Pastor Dalton concluded.

Tiffany approached Pastor Dalton after church services to discuss an uncomfortable subject. "Pastor Dalton, I was moved by your sermon today. It really hit home with a problem that I'm dealing with…Is it possible if I could talk with you…right now?"

"Certainly, young lady. Usually, I always ask one of the older sisters in the church to assist with certain matters. Do you mind?"

"Of course not," she responded apprehensively.

Pastor Dalton noticed Sister Armstrong standing nearby and beckoned for her to join the conversation. "Sister Armstrong do you have a few minutes to join me and Sister Guillory in my office. She has a problem that she would like to discuss and you know that I always like to have one of my trusty members to help with certain problems."

"Of course, Pastor; anything you ask. You know I'm always

willing to pray and console the young ladies in the church and guide them in the ways of the Lord," Sister Armstrong rattled on and on while eyeing Tiffany from the corner of her eye and plastering a smirk on her face.

Tiffany smiled, in turn, with a smirk and thought, *Oh no, not you. Ms. Holy-Thou-Art on Sundays, Pull the One Arm on Fridays.*

The trio proceeded to Pastor Dalton's office; the shelves were lined with books on topics relating to holiness, faith, grief, worry, and redemption. An oversized picture of the Lord rising up in to Heaven hung behind his desk, which was laden with family portraits. He motioned for the ladies to sit at the round mahogany table.

Tiffany was uncomfortable with Sister Armstrong in the room, especially after each of their confrontations in the ladies' room. But she slowly began to confess to the both of them the fact that she had been involved with a married man. Tears flowed freely down her freckled cheeks as the words stumbled out of her mouth. With each tear that fell upon her face, she felt the tension ease away and the heaviness of the shame lighten.

The harsh reality that Robert was a married man had taken its toll on her. She had vowed never to become involved in a tangled web of deceit. She struggled each day to move forward and put the painful ordeal in the past. The scene repeated constantly in her mind gnawing at her conscience piece by piece. She tried desperately in vain to erase the memory of meeting Robert's wife. Her sweet, innocent voice echoed in her mind. Her bubbly personality bounced back and forth.

"Well, Ms. Tiffany, we all make mistakes," Pastor Dalton interrupted her.

"Yes, we do," Sister Armstrong added. She handed Tiffany a box of Kleenex.

"Now, I'm not condoning what you did, but don't let this upset you. Learn the lesson. You don't have to look for love in the arms of a man. You can look for love from the Lord. He will always love you and be there for you."

Tiffany sat sobbing while she listened to Pastor Dalton's comforting words. She never had a father figure, or any man, to show her love or compassion. The words that Mr. Fontenot told her also continued to resonate in her mind, *Be careful of the company keep.*

"Remember you are beautiful young lady with a bright future. Allow God to bring the right man into your life at the right time. Trust me you will know when he is the right one," Pastor Dalton added. He gently smiled at her for added assurance.

"I thought I did know. He was sweet and kind. But now, when I look back, I see the red flags. Even my mama told me that there should be more to our relationship and that we didn't spend enough time together and that I'm supposed to be number one in his life." She dabbed at the tears forming in the corners of her eyes.

"Listen to your mama honey. She's right," Sister Armstrong stated with sympathy. "Everything is going to be ok. Like Ruth, your Boaz will show up. And he will love you and take care of you and provide for you. Remember he will find you." Sister Armstrong grabbed Tiffany's hand and squeezed it gently.

"Yes ma'am," Tiffany stated with a soft whimper. At this point, she did not have the strength to battle Sister Armstrong; however, it did not seem like it was necessary. Tiffany experienced a completely different person in Sister Armstrong; not the condemning and accusing woman that paraded around the church on Sunday mornings. She questioned if she was pretending to be caring, since they were with Pastor Dalton.

"Sister Armstrong, why don't you remain in touch with Ms. Tiffany so you can pray together? And continue to help her learn to trust in the Lord to strengthen her, love her, and restore her."

"Yes sir that is a wonderful idea. Why don't we start today? We can go to the prayer room and talk to the Lord before we leave the church," Sister Armstrong offered as she extended her hand to Tiffany.

"Ok. I would like that. Thank you Sister Armstrong," Tiffany responded uneasily. This was all so new to her – an understanding, nonjudgmental Sister Armstrong, trusting people who were not her family, and feeling the release of sickly shame.

They bowed their heads in prayer. Sister Armstrong invoked the Lord's presence into the small, secluded room, "Oh Father, we call on you in this hour of need for Ms. Tiffany. She needs ya Lord. Please Heavenly Father forgive her transgressions and sins, Lord, for she know not what she do."

Tiffany began to feel the presence of God surrounding her, then filling her soul, removing the guilt, shame, and conviction. She could feel the Lord binding those dual, dark demons of shame and rejection that had haunted her since her childhood days. She had stopped listening to Sister Armstrong and started listening to the calming, soothing, loving voice within her heart that said she is free, loved, and saved. Receive my grace and mercy – the twins of salvation.

The discussion with Pastor Dalton, and the prayer with Sister Armstrong, led her to resolve the issue immediately. Robert had rung her phone constantly since the humiliation she had suffered at lunch, but she had refused to answer. Now, Tiffany called Robert after she arrived back at her apartment. She dropped her purse on the sofa. She padded her way to the phone and dialed his number.

"Hello," Robert answered.

"Robert, you need to stop calling me. I don't want to have anything else to do with you. How could you lie?" She immediately stated her point. She did not want to waste time nor loose her courage to say what she needed to say.

"Tiffany, I'm sorry. I didn't lie. You never asked me if I was I married?" He attempted to use his savvy business skills to manipulate her and the conversation to defray any faults from himself.

"Oh, so this is my fault. You never should have approached me and asked for my phone number in the first place," she responded sharply.

"You're right, but you're so pretty. I just wanted to talk with you…but things started to heat up, so I kept the relationship going."

"But that was not fair to me or to your wife. I really thought you wanted to be with me. My feelings for you were growing. And now I've a lost whole lot – my job, my reputation…"

Robert cut her off. He did not want to hear the truth, and have to admit to her and to himself the grave mistake that he made. "You're right. I realize my mistake now and I'm paying for it dearly."

"Well it serves you right. So, don't call me anymore. It is over. Goodbye," Tiffany stated emphatically and hung up the phone. She did not want to hear anything else he had to say.

Monday morning arrived too soon for Tiffany. The bittersweet release of confiding in Pastor Dalton and Sister Armstrong still rang loud and clear in her mind.

She noticed the seasons changing in her life. Spring – fresh flowers, warm breezes. Summer – dry air, hot sand. Fall – orange leaves, crisp wind. Winter – frosty snowflakes, barren lands. Mama always said our lives are parallel to the seasons of the earth, changing at the precise time set forth by destiny. Life seasons, oftentimes, did not follow the pattern of Mother Nature's cycle of seasons.

Tiffany's life bypassed the stillness and serenity of summer and jumped right into the brittleness of fall. Everything was dropping to the ground, turning brown, and crumbling underneath her feet. Sometimes destiny will walk up and slap you in the face forcing you to wake up. Sometimes destiny will fall into your path like a rock causing us to stumble.

"Hey girl where were you yesterday? Why weren't you at church?" Tiffany phoned Jackie to inquire about her absence from church.

"I was tired. I've had a lot on my mind." Jackie responded as she sprawled out in her bed. She called in sick, which was rare for her to take time off. Even while suffering with the flu, Jackie pushed her self to go to work.

"Yes, I've noticed. You haven't been yourself lately." Tiffany padded her way to kitchen to brew a pot of coffee. She unfolded the Sunday newspaper on the kitchen table to the unemployment section to continue her job search.

"The nightmares keep coming back...then there is the drama with Kevin."

"You still haven't talked things over yet?"

"Somewhat. It's me. I don't want to deal with it. I don't know how to deal with it." Jackie pulled the covers over head to mask out the light and to hide from the facing the truth.

"How are you doing? I thought my ordeal was bad, but yours is like wow. A married man and now no job!" She wanted to change the subject and not talk about her drama.

"Thanks for saying it like that...I really feel better after that comment. I'm looking through the help wanted ads now. But any way yesterday, after church services, something interesting happened."

"What happened? Did Sister Armstrong show out?" Jackie threw back the comforter and sat up ready to hear some good gossip.

"Actually no, she didn't show out...she was very nice. I was so moved by Pastor Dalton's sermon that I talked with him after church about the Robert fiasco. And he invited Sister Armstrong in on the conversation. She was very pleasant and understanding."

"No you didn't!" Jackie exclaimed.

"Yes, I needed to talk with someone and learn how to release this guilt. Believe me...I didn't want to talk with Sister Armstrong, but once the Holy Spirit moves you...there is no turning back."

"What happened?" Jackie asked in amazement.

"I just told them everything that happened. Both of them were very understanding and comforting. Sister Armstrong prayed for me. I feel much better, but I know there is still more work to do...more healing."

"I know girlfriend. I'm right there with you. Kevin and I are preparing for our ski trip in a couple of months. It'll soon be one year since we met."

"I can't believe it has been a year," Tiffany replied halfheartedly.

"Have you heard from Robert?"

"He called a few times. Yesterday, I finally called to tell him not to call me anymore."

"What did he have to say?"

"He apologized for lying and hurting me. He said that he and his wife had been on shaky grounds. So, when we met, it was a nice change of pace."

"Whatever!"

"Now that I think about how things moved along, and especially his comment that I reminded him of someone, I assumed it was someone from his past. Lesson learned…never assume anything."

CHAPTER 16 - TURBULENCE

The fluffy clouds floated by as flight no. 247 to Denver sped along the sky's highway. The Boeing 757 was filled to capacity with passengers eager to start their Thanksgiving holiday. Jackie gazed out of the round hole that made up the window watching the blue sky as they jetted across the heavenly highway. Kevin relaxed in the leather blue seat and listened to some jazzy beats while he read the latest issue of *Money* magazine.

The flight attendant worked her way up the aisle taking beverage orders from the passengers.

"Would you like something to drink?" The airline attendant asked interrupting Kevin's bobbing head to the music. Jackie nudged Kevin in the side to get his attention. The earphones were glued to his ears to shield out the noise he did not want to hear.

"I'll have a Coke, please," Kevin responded to the flight attendant. He smiled at Jackie and pecked her check with a quick kiss.

"And you ma'am, what may I offer you?"

"I'll have a Sprite, thank you," Jackie replied and then smiled politely at Kevin in response to his subtle affection.

Their relationship had been on shaky grounds and had hit rock bottom ever since the mudslide happened in New Orleans. She loved him and wanted to spend the rest of her life with him but there was still the uncertainty. She had her doubts about his fidelity as well as her ability to trust him. She doubted the love he showed her, were any of the displays of affection genuine. She knew that she had on insecurities about men to tackle, and the ordeal with Kevin's infidelity added to the mountain of mistrust that had grown over the years.

She once thought the relationship was headed for the altar of Holy Matrimony, as fast as the Boeing 757 was flying through the sky. Jackie's head was in the clouds when it came to Kevin, but his exposed infidelity snapped her into the reality that their relationship was not perfect, and neither was she.

The preparation for the hopefully, joyous weekend went smoothly. They planned every detail together, and even had shopped together – something that Kevin did not particularly enjoy, but he shopped anyway. He knew how much Jackie loved to shop, and she could shop for hours. Jackie and Kevin had purchased ski clothes, jackets, gloves, hats, and sweaters. They had made numerous trips to different stores, throughout the metroplex, searching for all the right gear. The airline tickets were purchased, the hotel suite was booked, and the rental car was reserved. Kevin spared no expense hoping the vacation would help rebuild their trust in each other again.

Jackie shopped for warm clothes for the day and hot lingerie for the night. She focused all of her energy on not thinking about him sleeping with another woman. She focused on opening herself up to trust him again. Her emotions were twisted like a tin metal can spinning in a tornado. But the trip fueled excitement and added a burst of energy that was long overdue in their relationship. The vacation was planned for the couple to enjoy, not only the slopes, but each other for five days and nights. The weekend offered an abundance of time to mend their broken relationship without the distractions of cell phones, pagers, television, family, and friends.

They arrived at the busy Denver International Airport, picked up the rental car, and drove the two-hour long drive to Vail. The drive up into the snow-capped mountains was beautiful. Jackie read the signs – *Falling Rock, Crossing Deer.* They laughed nervously each time. The tension built up inside each of them from the rocky slopes and the rocky relationship.

"What do you want to do first after we check in?" Kevin asked as he drove the metallic blue Ford Taurus along the black-top highway. Driving this large family car was new for him. He was accustomed to speeding and quickly maneuvering in his sporty ride on the big city streets.

"First thing is eat. The peanuts served on the airplane are not going to keep the hunger pains away any longer," Jackie commented while playing with the radio to find a station with some decent music.

"Is that your stomach I hear growling? Kevin asked jokingly. "Girl, I'll find you some food quick, before you start chewing on me!"

"You're so funny!" Jackie replied. "Where are your CDs? I can't find anything worthwhile listening to on this radio."

Kevin pointed to his brown leather backpack and instructed Jackie to look in the outer zipped pocket. She reached in, pulled out the Brian Cole CD, and inserted the CD into the player. The first song to play was 'All Night Long.' Jackie thought w*hy did I play that CD?* All the memories of that explosive night in New Orleans flooded her mind. As the song played, she grappled with the decision to either discuss the infidelity issue in detail, to take this time to work things out and get to the bottom of the issue. Or just continue to let the problem simmer beneath the surface and eventually come to a full boil. Even though, they discussed Theresa briefly, they had not engaged in a heart-to-heart about why Kevin dated her at the same time, where is their relationship headed, and how can they mend their relationship to make it stronger?

"As I listen to this song, it brings back the memories of that night when I was in New Orleans," Jackie stated uneasily. She shifted restlessly in the seat.

Kevin gripped the steering wheel even firmer than he had

when turning one of the icy corners. He swallowed hard and thought long before responding to her comment.

"Why did you date her while dating me? Was it something I did or didn't do?" Jackie felt like she was sitting on pins and needles. But the scene was stitched in her mind, and she needed to unravel the painful truth.

"Well honestly...there were times when you pushed me away...like you didn't want to be bothered or you didn't want to be with me,"

"My actions were not intentional. I never wanted to push you away or make you feel like I didn't want to be with you," Jackie replied. Her voice was light and uncertain. She had to face the painful truth that she did not want to be rejected. But the very fact of rejection that she had tried to avoid surfaced and came to a full head.

"Well, if it was not intentional, what then?" Kevin asked confused and frustrated. "I tried to be loving and attentive and do what was right for our relationship. It was not my intention to cheat on you. But she was sweet and attentive, so I asked her out and one thing lead to another. I never meant to hurt you."

"I know deep down that you do love me. And I have to reach a point to be able to accept that love...and respect that love. Yes, I have to admit that at times I did push you away. There are so many mixed up emotions I have. You know that I lost my parents when I was a little girl. But I never told you that I was molested," Jackie let out a deep sigh. She needed to catch her breath. She looked straight ahead out the front car window, not able to look at Kevin as she shared the ugly truth.

Kevin reached over to hold her hand. He lifted her hand to his lips and tenderly kissed the back of her cold hand. "I understand that can be a painful ordeal. I can't imagine what you must be feeling or what you're going through."

"It has not been easy. I wish there were some magic words to make it all disappear, but the reality is that it happened. And I've come to realize that often times, it interferes with my relationships.

Trusting people is a big problem, and when someone betrays that trust, well the problem grows exponentially. So when I found out about Theresa, it drove me insane. All I could think about was 'How could he?' I didn't want to think about my own shortcomings or how I could be at fault."

"I'm happy that you shared your painful story with me. It really helps me to understand what you're going through and how you're feeling. And I apologize for adding even more hurt for you to deal with. I will try my best to make this weekend the best time you have ever had in your lifetime." Kevin stated.

They finally arrived in the coal miner's town, filled with the old world charm of the gold rush days, sprinkled with chic art galleries and clothing shops.

Kevin drove up to the ski lodge and parked in the garage. The couple walked hand in hand to the lobby adorned with rustic décor. The walls had a faux log cabin finish, the stuffed moose head hung over the giant fireplace, Native American designed rugs stretched across the floor, and a huge soft brown leather sofa sat perched in front of the fireplace.

"I know are you hungry," Kevin stated.

"I'm starving."

"How about I cook dinner for us tonight so we can enjoy each other's company and this wonderful suite? We can have a romantic candlelit dinner."

"Oh, I love it. Sounds perfect. After all, it's dark and late. I'm sure you're tired and want to unwind anyway," Jackie stated. The two embraced in a hug and held on to each for a moment. Kevin passed his fingers through Jackie's long locks. He loved the feel of her soft, silky hair.

The pair drove to a nearby grocery store and purchased steaks, potatoes, and a bottle of Merlot, and of course, some candles to fire up the ambience. Kevin loved to cook and showcase his culinary skills. He purchased all of the gourmet ingredients for a four-course meal. However, baking desserts was not included on his resume of culinary skills, so hot fudge chocolate ice cream would have to suffice for dessert, along with whipped cream.

Back at the hotel nestled in their deluxe suite, Kevin heated up not only the kitchen, but the fireplace as well. He instructed Jackie to sit back and relax as he had everything under control. She did as instructed, plopped down on the cranberry-colored tweed couch, propped her feet on the honey-oak coffee table, and flipped through the latest issue of *Essence* magazine. Kevin poured each of them a glass of Merlot, and then started his magic in the kitchen creating a tasty dinner.

Jackie tried to relax while she waited for Kevin to cook up his feast. She gazed at the same page in the magazine while her mind wandered if she did the right thing by confiding in Kevin about her traumatic past. She had never felt comfortable or inclined to open up and explain what happened those many years ago to anyone. But she knew eventually that the skeletons would protrude through the surface and come to the light. She prayed that she made the right decision. She knew in her heart that God would not steer her in the wrong direction. She did feel a sense of relief after confiding in Kevin. The built up tension melted away like ice cream melting in the hot sun. The shield of perfectionism crumbled and the armor of truth was erected. Jackie now knew that truth brings forth truth.

Kevin banged pots and pans. He clanked plates and glasses. The noise distracted Jackie from her lone thoughts. She padded her way to the kitchen to offer her assistance.

"Hey honey, do you need any help?" Jackie asked as she walked up behind Kevin. She opened the oven door and aroma of the pepper-crusted steaks wafted up into Jackie's nostrils.

"I have everything under control. You know I'm the master chef!" Kevin exclaimed while throwing his arms up in air.

"Of course you are, baby. Everything smells delicious."

"I'm finishing up the baked potatoes. I know you like extra butter. And I made sure that the rolls are extra soft, just for you," Kevin stated. He set the table, lit the candles, and dimmed the lights.

He then took Jackie by the hand, led her to the table, and pulled her chair out.

"Let's make a toast," Kevin smiled as he raised his wineglass.

"What are we toasting to?" Jackie asked as she raised her glass also.

"Here is to a new beginning!" They clicked there glasses and the chime sounded like the ringing of an angel's bell.

"A new beginning," Jackie reiterated. "I like that. Grandma Meme always said that to me whenever I was depressed. She told that when I went to live with after mama and daddy's car crash that was her new beginning. I was her little helper."

"I wish that I could've met your Grandma Meme. She seems like she was a sweet, wise lady."

"She was. I miss her so much," Jackie said with a hint of loneliness in her voice.

After feasting on their dinner, the couple plopped down on the sofa and watched a scary movie. Kevin removed his black ribbed turtleneck, and sported his white t-shirt. He placed his warm arm around Jackie's neck, so that her head was planted softly on his muscular chest. She covered her legs with the fuzzy crème-colored blanket that she had packed for extra warmth.

The two of them dozed off before the movie ended while snuggled in each other's arms. The long drive, the delicious meal, and the crackling fireplace set the tone for much needed relaxation and rest.

The next morning, the mountains greeted them protruding majestically thousands of feet above the earth. The snow blanketed the earth like a plush white carpet. The snow-capped pine trees stood erect lined along the side of the mountains. They ate breakfast quickly, draped themselves in their ski gear and headed to the slopes for their ski lessons.

The slopes were speckled with old and young decked out in a

rainbow of colors. Everyone either carried a snowboard or skies heading for the ski lift. Kevin and Jackie met up with their ski instructor and class.

"Hi, my name is Kevin and this is Jackie," Kevin extended his hand to the ski instructor while Jackie waved a quick hello.

"Hi, you guys. My name is Bo. Glad the two of you could join us. We're about to go over basic start and stop techniques."

Kevin and Jackie lined up with the other couples to take their turn practicing their moves. There was Tom and Alice, who were celebrating their tenth year anniversary. And John and Sara, who wanted to start a new holiday tradition. Everyone seemed to learn quickly the techniques that Bo effortlessly demonstrated, except Jackie.

She had never skied before and her lack of coordination was not helping things. Kevin became frustrated and embarrassed by her being the slow one in the class. She eventually progressed enough to ride the ski lift to the top of the beginner's mountain. Jackie's nerves were on edge. The sight of the trees spotted along the mountain that she had to ski down terrified her. All that she had heard in the news recently were about people who skied into a tree, some to an untimely demise or some were fortunate enough to only suffer a broken leg. She was sweating with nervous perspiration, even though the temperature registered at thirty degrees. She unzipped her violet parka to allow the cold air to seep in and cool her down. Kevin bumped her shoulder to help her relax and smiled his huge funny grin. She looked at and smiled nervously.

They reached the top of the mountain and the moment arrived for them jump of their seat and glide down the slope. Jackie glided for about ten feet before she landed firmly on her rear end. Kevin was already well ahead of her, skiing like an Olympic athlete, swishing from side to side. Jackie could see his red jacket zipping across the hill, while she unsuccessfully attempted to stand to her feet. Bo noticed her struggling and helped her to feet. He guided her down the mountain where they met up with Kevin.

"Hey, what took you so long?" Kevin asked.

"You know this is not my cup of tea," Jackie stated exasperated.

"Come on, give it another try. Then we'll have lunch. I noticed a neat restaurant located at the top of the mountain," Kevin said wanting to encourage her to try again. He removed his black ski glove and gently stroked her cheek with the back of his warm hand.

The next morning Jackie pleaded with Kevin, "Honey, this ski thing is just not for me. I'm a Southern girl. I'm enjoying myself, but my body is achy and tired. You go on without me today." Jackie wrapped her arms around Kevin's neck. She looked into brown eyes hoping he would understand.

"Are you sure?"

"Positive." Jackie had already planned her shopping route and mapped out the stores she wanted to peruse.

"Ok. I'll catch up with you later. And work on those achy muscles!" Kevin did not hesitate to leave. He wanted to enjoy as much time with Jackie, but he realized skiing was not the answer. He thought maybe the time apart would help. He would ski and she would shop.

Shortly after Kevin departed, Jackie dressed in her parka lined with a fur collar, her black form-fitting ski pants, and fleece-lined ski boots. She perused the quaint cottage shops, which lined the coal miner's town main street. Funny snow hats, picturesque postcards, metallic magnets, homemade jellies and jams, and broken Indian arrowheads lined the shelves in the shops.

She snapped photos of the mountains painted against the backdrop of the blue sky, the slivery creek that cascaded through the boulders, and the statues of the indigenous wildlife, to satisfy the amateur photographer inside of her. She felt at peace by herself; no tension and no worrying about pleasing someone else.

Later that day the two met up and decided to enjoy a walk in the evening twilight. The snow glistened like sparks of silver in the glow of the moonlight. Walking hand in hand and playfully bumping into each other, Jackie and Kevin smiled and kissed tenderly. They wrapped their arms around each other in a bear-like hug.

"Jackie, I know we can work through this," Kevin commented interrupting their playtime. Jackie sighed, a faint sigh of relief.

The couple walked back to their hotel. This was their last night in the cold miner's town. The days had been blanketed with crystalline snow, wind chills below zero, and crisp blue skies. The nights were embraced with tender moments and warm-hearted talks.

The pair arrived back at their suite. "I promised you earlier that I would work on your aching muscles," Kevin stated with wide smile spread across his face. Jackie just smiled and followed his lead. They threw their jackets, hats, and gloves on the sofa. He lit the fireplace, poured the wine, and started the whirlpool bathtub. A trail of clothes lined the path leading to the oversized bathroom. The two submerged into the hot, bubbly water and commingled their wet body parts. They washed and caressed each other's moist bodies kneading out the tension that was locked in their tight muscles.

The twosome surfaced from the whirlpool and followed the trail of clothes to the fireplace. Jackie did not bother with adorning herself with the sexy lingerie she purchased. They were beyond that moment. Kevin spread out the fuzzy crème-colored blanket and the couple wrapped themselves in each other's warm arms.

CHAPTER 17 - TRAVELING WITH TRUST

Pastor Dalton, poised with a serious demeanor, approached the podium filled with the Spirit, and ready to shepherd the saints into eternity. He read aloud the scripture reference of Proverbs chapter 3 verse 5 for his sermon. "Trust in the Lord with all your heart and lean not on your own understanding."

His voice bellowed into the microphone, "Saints you have heard the scripture reference for this morning's sermon. I want to use this as a title for this morning's message *Traveling with Trust.*"

The congregation shouted a few *amen's* and *well's* as Pastor Dalton straightened the eyeglasses that rested on his round, brown face. He sounded off into the microphone, "We walk down life's path, we reach a fork in the road, and we must make a decision. We cannot just stand there continuously contemplating what should I do. We must decide and progress towards the purpose God has destined for our very lives. When we walk down life's path, not trusting God, our surroundings are dark and dreary. Can I get an amen church?" Pastor Dalton asked.

"We feel lost and alone, but with pride riding high, we deny and suppress these feelings of loss and loneliness. We have that feeling that we are in control." Pastor Dalton's voice vibrated with his usual melodious tone of rise and fall on the right words. The congregation rose and sat in harmony with the sermon like a grand symphony.

"Now, the first road we travel in life is lonely, and often times leads to a dead end. It is at those times we must turn around and start over. We must start over with God as our guide, with him in control. For you see saints, when we surrender to God's will, we see a brighter day. We see the sun shining through the clouds lighting our paths. When we let God guide us in life, we come out on the other side in a better place. We come out of the wilderness of feeling lost and alone. And we come into the garden of peace and serenity. We come into the place where we can travel with trust in God. He is the captain of our ship, if you want to travel by sea; the captain of our airplane, if we choose to fly the friendly skies; and he is the conductor pumping the steam in the train's engine." Pastor Dalton paused for a sip of water. He blotted the perspiration that had formed on his brow.

He then continued with, "Oftentimes, we also reach a point in our lives when we begin to question 'what purpose I have? Why am I here?' God's word, in Matthew chapter 6 verse 33, reminds us to 'seek ye first the kingdom of God, and His righteousness; and all these things shall be added unto you.' Seeking God's face, first and foremost, through prayer, provides divine direction that will ultimately lead us to our purpose in the kingdom and in the earth," He exclaimed as the volume in his voice began to rise and strengthen.

"Saints, I instruct you to reflect upon the words 'and all these things shall be added unto you.' These words reveal that once God's kingdom and righteousness has been pursued as our initial purpose, then He will reveal the secondary purpose that each of us has. Purpose or "these things" revolves around the talents and gifts that the Holy Spirit has instilled in each of us. There are many gifts and talents that have been planted in each of us that will blossom in the proper season. When we use our gifts, the beautiful harvest will bring glory to our Father in Heaven and will be shared with fellow believers in the kingdom to bless and uplift them." Members of the congregation began to stand, shout, wave their hands, and shake their heads in agreement with the pastor's words.

"We cannot expect our purpose to surface overnight. Remember, the gardener plants in one season and the flowers bloom in another season. Manifested purpose is a growth process rooted in prayer. Therefore my friends do not fret with frustration. Remember to weed out worry and to consciously uproot anxiety by remaining focused on your initial purpose; to seek the kingdom of God. Allow the master gardener, the cultivator of your purpose, to plow the soil, to plant the seed, and to produce your fruit of purpose in due season."

The congregation wrapped themselves in Pastor Dalton's words like sheep wrapped in their own wool. *Amen's* echoed. *Hallelujah's* reverberated. *Yes Lord's* rang aloud. Some saints were so wrapped up in the sermon that an audible sound could not be mouthed, only an *ummhh*.

Sister Armstrong ran to the altar with arms flapping over her head like tree branches rattling in the wind. She hugged the altar's railing as if a strong gust of wind from the south would blow her out of the church. Her gambling demon danced around her soul for the victory it had won Friday night. Sister Armstrong had made her monthly pilgrimage to the Shreveport casino even after she had prayed for forgiveness and redemption. The Spirit moved, walls tumbled down, fears eroded, and demons died. Pastor Dalton's sermon had touched the core of her nerves. She had fallen by the wayside and not prayed to seek God's direction. She had prayed to win big at the Black jack table.

CHAPTER 18 - FATHER FIGURES

"Jackie, what is the status on the Anissá account?" Mr. Bell buzzed Jackie's office to inquire.

"I'm finalizing the analysis of the market research," Jackie responded. She placed her hands on her head frustrated that her performance at work had slipped below par. She knew that her performance on this account could either elevate her career to the next level or she could crash and burn.

"I need those figures on my desk first thing in the morning," Mr. Bell instructed.

"Yes sir," Jackie looked at the time on her computer and five o'clock was fast approaching. She realized this was going to be a long night. Her career was at stake so she had to focus all of her attention on this account.

Jackie dialed Kevin's number. "Hi sweetie, I have to work late. I won't be able to make our date tonight."

"What do you mean? You've known about this company dinner for weeks."

"I know. But I have to finish the analysis report to give to Mr. Bell first thing in the morning. I'm sorry. What would you do if you were in my shoes?" Jackie already knew the answer; he would cancel any plans they had.

"Yeah…I'll talk with you later," Kevin responded wanting to impress guilt upon Jackie. But he knew that his career was number one and everything else was second. She hung up and just stared at the phone for a minute thinking, how dare him. She shuffled the papers on her desk and attempted to focus on the task at hand.

She usually attended all of his events – business or social – as the dutiful girlfriend, who hoped to be his wife, if he ever popped the question. She smiled and charmed all of his colleagues as well as his superiors. But right now her career was on the line and Kevin would have to ride in the backseat. She focused all of her attentions on her goals, her dreams, and her success. She prayed that the Lord would lead her and give her the strength and wisdom to make the right decision to keep their relationship on the right track. The lines of communication were opened after confiding in Kevin about her traumatic past, and especially, since he expressed concern and empathy. The apology about his affair with Theresa also helped. But she still had to work one day at a time to keep the nightmares away. The process of healing was not an easy one. She realized opening up to Kevin was only the beginning.

Jackie printed the report, reviewed the numbers, and realized that the data was skewed. She brought the report to the Mr. Bell's office. Luckily, he had not left for the day.

"Mr. Bell, I have worked on the data all day, and it is still not populating correctly," Jackie stated with earnest desperation.

Mr. Bell looked at Jackie, his best employee and noticed her frustration. Jackie was the one employee he could count on to provide accurate information. Obviously, something was wrong that caused distress in his top performing employee.

"Give me the report and have a seat. We'll work through it until it's correct. I need to present the data tomorrow to the company's representative." Mr. Bell loosened his necktie and started reviewing the numbers.

Jackie did not know how to respond her boss's comments. She knew that lately she had slacked off. She exerted more pressure on herself than anyone else. She still had pieces of perfectionism that surfaced.

"What's wrong Jackie? Usually you are top of things. I would have had this report from you over a week ago," Mr. Bell asked with genuine concern in his voice while glaring over the top of the report.

"I'm ok. Just a lot on my mind. I promise not to let my personal life interfere with my work." Jackie sat on the edge of the chair in front of Mr. Bell's oversized mahogany desk.

"Well it happens to the best of us. We are human and not perfect. You know that whenever you need help, just ask." He stated while leaning back in oversized black leather chair. Everything in his office was oversized. Everything was king-sized, the desk, chairs, windows, pictures, especially since; Mr. Bell was a king-sized man. When Jackie stood next to Mr. Bell, it was like David standing in front of Goliath.

Jackie and Mr. Bell worked tirelessly until the numbers added up correctly. The time ticked by quickly and dinnertime was approaching quickly. They ordered a large meat-lovers pizza, from Sal's Pizzeria, to curve the hunger pains. Mr. Bell continued to press Jackie to open up about her concerns. He needed his best employee in tip top shape.

"Is it work that has you stressed out?"

"No, sir. It's personal. Restless nights, relationship problems. I'm not up to talking about it. I promise that I'll handle it and not allow my problems to interfere with my work." Jackie replied with as much confidence in her voice that she could muster.

"I know that you are a hard worker and one of my best employees. Life throws us curve balls to knock us off our path, but we have to keep dodging the balls. And know that this will pass. You're a tough cookie so don't let life knock you down. Remember to always get back up, press on, and when you are weary, rest awhile. We all need rest. When the Anissá account is completed, take some time off."

"I will. Thank you for understanding and the words of wisdom, and especially the time off," Jackie stated smiling faintly.

She gathered her papers and cleaned up her desk. The clock on her desk registered 8:16 pm. She grabbed her black trench coat and raced for the elevator. It was still early enough to meet up Kevin at his dinner. She pushed the speed dial button for his cell phone number, his voicemail answered.

"Hi, sweetie. I finished working on my project and was calling to meet up with you. But since I couldn't reach you, I'm heading home. Call me later."

Tiffany stretched out on her couch while channel surfing to enjoy a relaxing Sunday afternoon. The heavy food from Sisters Souls weighed her down. She enjoyed lounging in her pink yoga gear. She only worked out to her yoga DVD maybe once or twice. But the way she saw it, she did not need to exercise. She knew her body was young and sexy, since she was still turning heads. When the phone rang, she thought it was Jackie calling to recap the morning Sunday service. She reached over to the end table to pick up the receiver.

"Hello," Tiffany answered casually.

"Hello, Tiffany."

"Yes," Tiffany responded cautiously. She did not recognize the voice on the other end of the phone.

"It's Jack. I hope you don't mind, but I asked Robert for your phone number."

Tiffany sat up. "No, I don't mind. But I don't understand why you are calling me. I'm also surprised that he gave you my number, and even more surprised that he still had it."

"You've been on my mind since we met, that day, at the restaurant."

Tiffany was perplexed. She was not into dating men that old. She wandered what had Robert told him about their relationship.

"Do you remember when I said that you reminded me of one of my daughters?"

"Yes." Her face contorted with a confused expression.

"Do you remember when you asked me if I had ever eaten at Petre's?"

"Yes," Tiffany answered becoming annoyed with all of the questions.

"Do you remember when you asked me if I knew your mother, who worked at the café?"

"Yes." She replied exasperated.

"Well, I knew your mother very well...I knew Luella in a very special way."

"Ok. What do you mean? I asked her if she knew you and she said she didn't remember you." Tiffany held her other hand in air.

"Well...I called her shortly after meeting you. I called her to ask about you."

"You called my mother? How and why do you have her phone number? And what about me did you ask?" Tiffany fired off her line of questions.

"Well, I've her number for many years, and I'm glad that it hadn't changed," Jack then paused for a moment. "I asked her about...this is not easy. I asked her if you were possibly my daughter. Luella and I had a very special relationship just about as many years ago as what your age is."

"What do mean you had a special relationship? What kind of relationship?" Tiffany questioned. She had never conceived of the idea to ask her mother about the relationships that she had with men. The subject seemed inappropriate and taboo.

"I'm saying Tiffany that I'm your father." Jack gripped the telephone receiver tightly. He knuckles turned white. He held his breath waiting for a response. He hoped the response would be a positive one. He had waited for this moment for years.

"My what? My father. I think my mother would have told me that." Tiffany rubbed her hand through her hair.

"Yes, but your mother was very prideful and didn't want any interference or help from me, but I persisted. I gave extra money to Petre to give to Luella as bonus money. She'd already refused my help directly. And the race issue didn't help matters either. After all, Sunset is a small town and she wanted to move on with her life – just the two of you. So, eventually I moved on, got married, and started a family."

"I don't believe you." Tiffany stood up. The news was too much for her to remain seated calmly – her father calling her and the fact that he was a white man. She started pacing the floor treading a path back and forth across her shaggy rug. Oblivious to the fact that she knocked over the glass of Coke that was sitting on the floor in front of the sofa, she kept pacing back and forth.

"I know this sounds far-fetched, even ridiculous." Jack responded.

"But I talked to her and…she didn't say anything to me. I don't believe this…why wouldn't she tell me the truth? And why now are you calling me?"

"Tiffany, please believe me that I wanted to be a part of your life, but the circumstances were difficult. And I want to be in your life now…to be a father…the father you never knew."

Tiffany was silent. She stood in the middle of the floor with her arm wrapped around her waist. She could not believe that after all of these years of desiring to know who her father was that she was talking to him. All the years of curiosity if she looked like him, acted like him, smiled like him, had finally come to the light of day. She had long thought that she would recognize him in an instant like seeing her reflection in a mirror. Even though, her dreams had come true, she felt like the conversation was a dream.

"Tiffany, are you still there?" Jack asked with concern in his voice. "I know this is a shock, but it was as much a shock for me when I met you with Robert."

"Yes, I'm still here," Tiffany answered barely above a whisper.

"I would like for us to talk in person…to maybe try to catch up."

"Yeah…umm…maybe…I need to call my mother first."

CHAPTER 19 – TRUTH BE TOLD

Tiffany held the phone suspended in midair. The news sent shockwaves through her body like an earthquake measuring seven-points on the Richter scale. She was not able to fully comprehend the shocking revelation that Jack was her father. Tiffany snapped back to reality and phoned her mama for an unsettling confrontation.

"Mama, why didn't you tell me?"

"Tell you what? And what happened to *Hello. How are?*"

"Why didn't you tell me the truth about Jack Fontenot? He just called me."

Luella swallowed hard, rubbed her hand through her hair, and took a deep breath. The moment she hoped would never come had quickly arrived like unexpected labor pains. "Jack called you. How did he get your number?"

"From Robert, but that's not important. He said that he spoke with you, not too long ago, and told you that he had met me. I talked with you also and asked if you knew him…and you just blew me off…claiming you didn't remember."

"Sweetheart."

"Why Mama…why didn't you tell me?"

"It's complicated, sweetheart. We lived in a small town where, if you are from the wrong side of the tracks, then you don't mix with those on the other side. But we were attracted to each other. We had a secret affair. We were both young and crazy in love. Then I found out that I was pregnant and I broke it off. I avoided him until…well I started showing. My big belly protruded out to yonder. And when you were born, so pale and pink, fuzzy blonde hair, I knew everyone would talk, so I denied who the father was. I lied to everyone – even to myself."

"But why did you lie to me the other night?"

"I'm sorry sweetheart. I didn't think he would call you. I still wanted things to remain the same – uncomplicated, simple."

Tiffany continued to listened to her mother explain the years that had been lost, years of confusion, years of emptiness, and years of futile searching.

"When he found out I was pregnant, he offered to help. I didn't ask him to help. I didn't want to be a burden," Luella explained to Tiffany. "He helped because he felt obligated. Petre told me years later, just before he passed away, that Jack gave him money to give to me for you."

Tiffany remained silent listening to her mother talk about the man who was her father; the man who provided financial support, but never emotional support. The rumors were true. She was a half-bred, a mulatto, a person who had half an identity, now with a whole identity, to a certain degree. She wanted to ask her mama why she never told her about him before now; as if Luella was reading her mind.

"I wanted to tell you sweetheart, but the time never seemed right. Life was complicated enough just being a single mom. I didn't want to add extra troubles about who was your daddy." Luella spoke carefully like treading through deep, murky waters, and feeling consciously for every step. She wished Tiffany said something, anything to indicate what she was thinking and feeling.

"I wish you would have told me earlier," Tiffany mouthed with an emptiness echoing in her words. "I think that would have been more than fair, after all, I haven't been a child for a long time. All these years wandering and wishing to know who he was. Almost every day, every man I saw, I looked closely at his face searching to find a little piece of me in his face."

Tears began to stream down Luella's face as Tiffany spoke life to the anguish, the shame, and the disappointment that resided in her soul. Luella wiped away the tears that flowed down her round face with her thin fingertips. She wished that she could wipe away the hurt that Tiffany was feeling, but she knew that only time had the healing power to erase away the painful memories. Only time would bring peace and understanding. She prayed that time rushed in like the waves rolling onto the sandy shores that washed away the footprints in the sand.

Tiffany's mind was blank, her heart numb, and her soul cold. The last few months had been exhausting. She could not complete jumping over one hurdle before another one was fast approaching. The affair with Robert, the accidental meeting with her daddy, the confrontation with her mama; she wanted this race to end. She had no more to give, no more strength. She remembered the old wise saying that Jackie often repeated, passed down from her grandmother, *Life is a cycle of new beginnings*. She wanted and needed a new beginning without bumps in the road, a beginning down a lighted path, and a beginning where she could lean on, trust in, and be strong in God.

She did not know what else to say to her mama, except *good-bye*.

Tiffany hesitantly punched the numbers on the telephone pad. She wrestled with apprehension praying that she was doing the right thing. She nervously listened to each ring, the sound echoing in her ear. She kept her finger on the button to end the call, so if in the last instant her courage faded away. She heard the deep voice answer after what seemed like an eternity. Her mouth was a cottony dry and her words clung to the roof of her mouth. She finally managed to utter a faint word.

"Hello, Robert," she anxiously mouthed. Her heart thumped louder than a drummer banging on his snare drum.

"Tiffany?" Robert asked. "I'm shocked to hear your voice again, and may I add still sounding sweet."

"Yes, it's me. Are you busy?" She did not want to make small talk nor listen to his flirting.

"Never too busy for you." A smile crept across his face. "How may I be of service?"

"I'm calling about Jack. You gave him my phone number."

"Yes, I hope you didn't mind. He said he needed to get in touch with you...something about your mother. So I assumed it would be ok."

"Yeah, that's fine. He called me and told me that he and my mother were friends...well more than friends. It appears that they had a relationship...and he says that he is my father." Tiffany paused to catch her breath. She then thought *why am I sharing this intimate information with this jerk*. But she pressed forward on to the real reason for her phone call. "Do you have his phone number? I didn't write it down when he called." She held her breath again waiting for his response.

"Yes, of course I have it." Robert leaned over his desk and slowly thumbed through his rolodex wanting to prolong their conversation. "You know, Tiffany, I want to apologize for any hurt that I may have caused you because of my behavior."

"Uh huh, I'm listening," Tiffany responded half-heartedly. She tapped her fingers restlessly on the kitchen table.

"I'm still looking for the phone number." He stated to keep Tiffany's attention and not have her cut him off. "I never had a chance to tell you that...at the time we met, things were not so hot between me and Alysse."

"Uh huh, whatever you say. Have you found the phone

number, yet?" She responded sternly. She prayed that he would hurry up. As she listened to his voice, tiny ripples of leftover feelings surfaced. Even under the circumstances, her emotions could not be easily washed away.

"Still looking." Robert held Jack's business card in his hand. He attempted to prolong the conversation as long as he could. "You were just so pretty and sweet and charming that I forgot about everything else. I just wanted to meet and talk with you, then one thing lead to another..."

"Have you found the number?" She demanded. Her patience had subsided. She wanted to end the conversation quickly and not regret having called him. She had too many emotions tangled up inside her – she hated him for lying to her, but she appreciated him for his help.

"Yes, it is 318-436-5683. Tiffany could we..."

"Thanks. Good bye." She quickly cut him off, before he could propose anything else.

The phone call was quick and to the point. Her nerves were on edge during the entire conversation. They decided to meet on Sunday after church services at Trevino's, the place of their unintentional first meeting. Since Jack was not too familiar with the city, they agreed upon that location as the meeting spot. Jack scheduled his flight to arrive early Sunday morning hoping there would not be any flight delays. He had waited long enough to meet his oldest daughter. He had shared the information with Ilene, his wife of twenty-three years, that he had finally made contact with Tiffany. He had informed her long ago about the relationship between him and Luella, and that they had a daughter. However, Luella had kept him at a distance from participating in their daughter's life.

The long awaited day had arrived for her and Jack to meet in person – one on one. She prayed that the dreams she had envisioned, throughout the years of their first meeting, were finally going to see the light of day. In her dreams, everything was perfect – a happy reunion of father and daughter filled with lots of laughter, warm hugs, and friendly kisses.

Tiffany scoured through her closet a dozen times searching for the perfect outfit. She wanted to look her best, to look like a daughter, the daughter that he wanted to meet. She finally decided to wear something simple. She dressed in her navy knit dress, clasped on her string of pearls, and fastened her navy sling back shoes. She wanted to rectify the first impression he had of her when he had met her with Robert, and it did not help the situation any that their meeting was at the same restaurant. She thought as she dressed, *faith has a funny sense of humor.*

Tiffany sat in church watching the clock throughout the entire service. She prayed that Pastor Dalton would preach one of his quick sermons, but it seems like her prayers were not answered. To Tiffany, it felt like he preached about eternity, from the creation to the second coming, not leaving out any details. At last, the benediction was spoken. She shook hands and said a few hellos. She told Jackie that she would call her later. She rushed from the church, drove quickly to the restaurant, and attempted to calm her nerves.

The freshness of fall lingered in the air outside. But in Tiffany's world, the newness of spring bloomed inside of her. Her emotions were like riding up and down on a rollercoaster – excited, nervous, happy, scared, and confident, confused.

The maître d' escorted Tiffany to the table where Jack sat waiting. She had a quick moment of déjà vous. He smiled excitedly when he noticed her walking towards him. He stood up and reached out to give her a hug. She hugged him back releasing some of the nervous tension that had built up inside of her. She exhaled then smiled.

"I've waited so long for this moment," Jack commented after they sat down.

"Really, so have I," Tiffany replied. She did not know what

else to say. All of the conversations that she had dreamed about suddenly escaped from her mind.

"You are so beautiful, just like your mother was so many years ago. And you look a lot like my daughters, Julie and Erica. I think I mentioned that before." Jack stared at Tiffany with a proud twinkle in his eyes.

"Thank you. I remember that you said that. Even though I want to forget about that day," Tiffany responded meekly. The waiter sat two glassed of water on the table and waited for their orders. They ordered quickly to continue with their conversation.

"Even though the circumstances were awkward and favorably, we more than likely would have never met," Jack stated to reassure her that he was not judging her.

"That's true. Well Robert and I are no longer friends. I found out about his wife among other things." Tiffany drank a sip of water. She wanted to avoid any eye contact after making that statement. He reached out to hold her hand for support.

"Changing the subject...we have a lot of catching up to do," Jack commented. "And I can't wait for you to meet my family. I've told them all about you and they are excited to meet you."

Tiffany listened to every word he said. She eyed his features observing his dusty blonde hair, sea blue eyes, pale skin, and thin lips. She had finally discovered the other half of her. The questions about her heritage had been answered. The words spoken about her many years ago from the teasing neighborhood children were true. Tiffany began to feel a sense of wholeness, completeness, and oneness.

"Yes, I would like to meet them," Tiffany responded uncertainly. The thought of having sisters had not entered her mind. She always had mama to herself, now that she had daddy, she would have to learn to share. Life as she knew it was changing. The door to the past had been unlocked and she had crossed the threshold into a new world comprised of new people.

The time passed quickly as father and daughter conversed to

catch up on the years they missed together. Jack had a flight to catch to return back to his family. It was a bittersweet departing, since the time was so short. But know since the truth was revealed and there was no turning back the hands of destiny, they vowed to talk daily to each other and to visit frequently.

CHAPTER 20 - ON THE HORIZON

Jackie pushed the number one on her cell to speed dial Kevin again later that night. "Hello, Kevin." She responded after he answered the phone. "How was the dinner?" She asked.

"Everything was great. The usual crowd and conversation. I wish you could've been there, but I understand about working. Were you able to work everything out and finish up your project?" Kevin asked as he stretched out on the black leather sofa in his loft apartment. He had the morning newspaper tossed around on the wood floor, the half-empty glass of diet Coke sat on the glass table, and stacks of magazine piled up in the corner.

"Yes, we were able to work everything out. I wish I could've been there with you."

"Who *is* we?" Kevin asked with a hint of jealous concern in his voice. A puzzled expression was plastered across his face.

Jackie thought it was her imagination that he sounded jealous. "Mr. Bell and I. He helped me work the numbers. If not, I would still be at the office." Kevin breathed a sigh of relief. "But I am going out of town for a couple of days. I need to go home, to Creekwater, and visit my parents and Meme's gravesite."

"Are you going by yourself? Do you want me to go with you?" Kevin asked with sincere concern.

"Yes, I'm going to drive by myself. I need the time to think and clear my head." Jackie responded. She sat cross-legged on the floor in her living room. She leaned her back on the sofa and gazed up at the ceiling.

"Are you sure you want to be by yourself? I can take some time off from work. I don't want you traveling that long distance by yourself. Anything could happen. I don't want to lose you. I love you."

"I love you, too, sweetheart. But trust me, I'll be fine. I've carried this burden all these years by myself, and now I need to release it by myself." Jackie responded. A single tear escaped the corner of her eye.

"When was the last time you visited Creekwater?"

"I haven't been home, since Meme passed away. There wasn't any reason for me to travel back there. I wanted to keep everything buried in the past. I thought by not going back home, I could escape from the pain, but I was wrong. So, I'm hoping that by visiting this time that I can confront the truth and bring it to the light of day…and maybe, I can move on with my life."

Jackie dressed in her heather-gray warm up suit, tied on her sneakers, and pulled her hair back into a flowing ponytail tucked underneath a baseball cap. Now was not the time for perfection - no fancy clothes, makeup, and curling iron. She tossed her overnight tote bag in the trunk along with the prized quilt that Grandma Meme had stitched long ago. She did not need much, just the necessities to carry her through the night.

She cranked up her Honda, shifted into gear, and started the drive well before the dawn peeked over the earth's edge. She drove the twelve hours to Creekwater without a thought to time or place. She only stopped for gas and quick trips to the restroom. She knew that time had come to speak the truth to the people who loved her dearly, and to the one person who hurt her deeply. As she sped along the lone, dark stretch of highway, her thoughts whizzed through her mind like a racing car speeding along the racetrack. She decided that she could not continue pretending that her life was perfect or that she had everything under control. It seemed like the tighter she tried to hang on, the quicker she fell. She felt like she was falling into that deep, dark sink hole, and there was bottom in sight.

She crossed the long bridge that stretched over Lake Eaton, marking the entryway into the rural town. The red, hot sun dipped below the earth's horizon casting a fiery glow across the evening sky of Creekwater. Streaks of gray clouds swirled across the Heavens leaving traces of a bittersweet day. The intermingling of colors in the sky resembled the conflicting emotions spinning within Jackie.

Population of five thousand. Years marked by progress had passed in her big-city world, but in the town of Creekwater, time did not change. Everything looked exactly as the day she left; the oyster house on the boardwalk, the corner stop and shop, the palm trees lined along the sandy shore, and cars driving by lazily at thirty miles per hour.

Jackie drove across the railroad tracks to the colored graveyard. She drove on the gravely driveway, which zigzagged throughout the graveyard, and parked the car near the family plot of burial land. The graveyard was spotted with a rainbow of flowers that was evenly dispersed throughout the pasture of land.

She grabbed the cherished quilt from the trunk of the car that had decorated the wall in her bedroom. She walked slowly toward the gravesites where her beloved family lay resting in peace.

As Jackie kneeled beside the neatly kept grave markers of her parents, and her beloved Meme, layers of shame slowly began to crack and peel away like a scab in its final healing stages. The wounds healed slowly like moving at a snail's pace. Slow and steady. Jackie felt like the life, which had been sucked out of her throughout the years, poured back into her with freshness and resiliency. A seed of strength planted, in the deep recesses of her soul, rooted and sprouted like the planting of an oak of righteousness. Steady and unyielding, stretching its roots wide and deep. The new planting yielded a new birth. *A new beginning.* The beginning that Grandma Meme had always talked about whenever Jackie was doubtful.

Jackie faced the slate gray grave markers with an absolute firmness to close the door on the past that created countless nights of nightmares and dreaded days of dismissal daydreams. The grave markers in the family plot stood erect under the maple tree.

HOWARD WESTON	DOROTHY WESTON	GRACE 'MEME' WESTON
1942 – 1987	1945 – 1987	1920 – 1999

Jackie spoke to the pillar of marble at the head of the green pasture where the remains of her mama rested. She spoke the words that had been silenced and the hurt that throbbed within her.

"Mama, I didn't know how to tell you what happened with Daddy. I thought it was best to keep quiet. I didn't want you to be mad with me. I didn't know if you would believe me or blame me. I didn't want you to make Daddy leave. I didn't know what to do. All of these years I have kept silent. I didn't even tell Meme. I didn't want to upset her. She loved Daddy just like you loved him. He was all she had after Grandpa passed away. I've kept silent until know, but I can't keep silent any longer. I don't know if you can hear me or if you're watching down from Heaven. I don't know if he is there with you. I'm trying to forgive him and move forward with my life. I keep going in circles...the same pain and hurt and anger...so much confusion.

"I remember the good times that you and I spent together. Shopping, cooking...or me trying to help with the cooking....baking chocolate chip cookies. I miss you, Mama, so much. Life hasn't been the same without you. Meme did a great job, as a fill in, but things still weren't the same. I miss her too. I miss her so much that I kept the quilt she made. I have a special place to hang it in my bedroom. I have it here with me. I know Meme made the quilt for Daddy, but it is also a part of Meme. Do I keep the quilt? Do I give it away? I'm confused. Good and bad memories are woven into the fabric. Maybe I'll put it in my special chest with the rest of my cherished possessions.

"I don't know if I should miss Daddy or not. I did love him…I still want to love him…to miss him. But I've come to realize that the pain he caused has stayed with me all these years; the bad dreams, sleepless nights, and lack of trust in other people, and even in myself. I don't know how to move forward with my life.

"I know Meme always said that *Life is a cycle of new beginnings.* Her words keep echoing in my mind. I try to mediate on those words to help me move forward, at least one day at a time. I miss you Mama. I miss you Meme."

After a long pause, Jackie was finally able to mouth the words, "I miss you Daddy…and I…I forgive you." Her mouth curved upward to form a faint, nervous smile. A small tear escaped the corner of her eye and rolled slowly down her cheek that marked the beginning of healing.

A cool, gentle breeze caressed her cheek and enveloped her body. She wrapped the quilt around her shoulders. At that moment, warm pleasant thoughts surfaced in her mind; thoughts of Meme and Mama, and even thoughts of Daddy.

Jackie realized that her memories lingered into her present and that the past is always with us. But we can release the weight of the memories that anchor us down to the past and, with determination and persistence, move forward to a fresh beginning.

Jackie left the graveyard just before darkness set in. She checked into the local roadside motel. The room was small and the air was stale. Her body was drained, her mind was blank, and her heart was empty. Jackie draped herself across the bed covered with a green flowered bedspread, and cried herself to sleep. The water from the tears continued to heal her hurt and to purge her pain.

CHAPTER 21 - FULL BLOOM

The Daughters at the Well bible study members arrived one by one. The group remained small to maintain intimacy and privacy. The weariness of their long days slowly began to fade as warm smiles, friendly hugs, and light laughter filled the room. Gospel music played softly in the background ushering in peace and serenity.

Sister Armstrong greeted everyone with a hug and a warm welcome. She had opened her heart and mind to accepting other's mistakes after her spiritual awakening to her own faults. She realized that salvation and healing has no age limits, nor does imperfections.

Tiffany finally decided to join the group after much encouraging by Sister Armstrong. Their prayers sessions helped to build a relationship of trust and respect between the two women.

Tiffany sat at the large oak table in the disciples' room in silent mediation before the class was called to order. Thoughts raced through her mind about the disappointments in her life. Everyone had disappointed her, including her mama. She had even disappointed herself.

She flipped through her notes on last Sunday's message, *Prayer Leads to Purpose*, and she heard a still, small voice whisper to her *trust me, follow me, love me and allow me to love you. You have the power that you need within you. You have my power. Embrace it, hold it, and use it.*

Jackie arrived just in time before the group started with the opening prayer. She sat next to Tiffany. She finally had learned how to appreciate waiting and the gift of patience. Patience made her life less complex, simpler. She enjoyed the comfort of knowing that that every waking minute did not have to be filled with a constant state of motion. She relaxed and enjoyed each blessed day. Loneliness and insecurity were buried in the grave six feet under a heavy slab of cement.

"Hey Tiff, what's up? Do you know what the topic is for tonight?" Jackie asked.

"Hey girl. It's about time you got here," Tiffany joked with Jackie. "The topic is praying for Jackie to be on time!"

"Whatever...I'm working on it. You know that when I become caught up at work and one thing leads to another," Jackie responded to defend her tardiness.

"I think Kevin's philosophy of tardiness is rubbing off on you," Tiffany continued joking.

"Ok, ladies we're going to start now with our opening prayer," Sister Armstrong stated to call everyone to attention. The group joined hands, bowed their heads, and listened to the prayer led by Sister Armstrong. "Tonight we'll discuss forgiveness. I know that most of us have had to forgive someone, even ourselves. We also have to learn to accept forgiveness. We'll each take our turn talking about a time when we had to forgive someone. Who wants to start?"

Tiffany raised her hand to start off the discussion. "I'll start. I had to learn to forgive myself. I blamed myself constantly sometimes knowingly and other times unknowingly for having an affair with a married man. I wanted so much to have that father figure in my life that I misjudged what was real love. I think that I was drawn to Robert because he was older and provided a sense of security and wisdom. I admit that it felt nice. So, I was blind to finding out the truth about him and his life. I heard only what I wanted to hear. I also had to learn to forgive my mother. I know she wanted to shield me from the truth that she thought would hurt me," Tiffany allowed her words to flow freely. Once she started talking, her words would not stop. She did not even allow herself to breathe during her much needed release of her emotions. To hear the words spoken aloud, provided a therapeutic healing.

Jackie started her forgiveness confession as soon as Tiffany had ended her confession. "I needed to forgive myself also. I blamed myself for the molestation by my father. I was young and didn't understand that I didn't do anything wrong. I had to learn to forgive my father for his misbehavior. The process has been long and hard. There are days when progress is happening, and then there are days when I revert back to feeling the shame and pain. And I had to learn to forgive Kevin for his infidelity and dishonesty," Jackie followed Tiffany's lead by allowing her words to flow freely along with the tears that stained her cheeks. Jackie grabbed hold of the power to forgive first herself, then everyone else.

The other three ladies made their individual confessions as the atmosphere was ripe for shedding layers of hurt, pain, and shame. They each peeled back layer after layer to reveal the purified core of truth. The healing process unfolded slowly over time. The veil of darkness was lifted from covering their hearts, and the light of forgiveness shone brightly. The full harvest had budded to penetrate through the surface, and pushed away disappointments, disillusionments, and disruptions. Yes, the harvest came – full of life, full of love, and full of laughter. The season of spring was in full bloom in the midst of winter.

"Ladies, this has been an awesome night for healing. Thank each of you for sharing your experiences. You have each released your past hurts and opened up yourselves to forgiveness on every level. Like the woman at the well, you have each received the grace of the living water," Sister Armstrong encouraged the ladies. She led the group in a closing a prayer.

CHAPTER 22 - LIGHT REFLECTED

Tiffany finally decided to devote herself completely to the Lord. Who else did she have to trust? Who else could she depend on? Who else could she turn to? Everyone had disappointed her, including her mama. She had even disappointed herself. Sitting in her bible study class and reading through her notes on last Sunday's message, Prayer Leads to Purpose, she heard the still, small voice whisper to her trust me, follow me, love me and allow me to love you. You have the power that you need within you. You have my power. Embrace it, hold it, use it.

The class members started to arrive one by one. The weariness of their long days slowly began to fade as the warm smiles, friendly hugs, and light laughter filled the room. Gospel music played softly in the background ushering in peace and serenity.

Tiffany glanced up from her notes. Her eyes met the gaze of the light brown eyes that had just entered the room. The church membership had grown so rapidly within a short time span that many fresh faces had cropped up overnight. She felt like the seed of destiny, which had been planted in her soul long ago, began to burst forth. The feeling was not from the heart. The heart can be deceitful at times. The feeling reverberated like destiny had just walked in the room and took a seat right next to her. Destiny walked in and closed the gap of loneliness, evicted rejection, and built a foundation of trust.

"Hello," as the smile behind his hello echoed in his eyes. His lips, the color of honey, spoke simply and plainly. The touch of his warm hand on her arm lit a spark. The full harvest budded and sprouted to penetrate through the surface, and pushed away disappointments, disillusionments, and disruptions. Yes, the harvest came – full of life, full of love, and full of laughter. The season of spring was in full bloom in the midst of winter.

"Hello," Tiffany said.

ABOUT THE AUTHOR

Pamela Pujo, author of **A Journey Through Time**, is a native of Louisiana and currently resides in the Dallas, Texas metroplex. Pamela enjoys reading, writing, acting, traveling, and of course, spending time with her family and friends. Her wish is to inspire others to actively pursue their dreams and to embrace their destiny. She believes that our gifts and talents are developed in stages during different phases of our lives. Each individual experience, great and small, prepares us for your destiny. So, enjoy the journey!

www.ingramcontent.com/pod-product-compliance
Lightning Source LLC
Chambersburg PA
CBHW061243170626
46809CB00007B/2813